BOOKS BY COLBY RODOWSKY

WHAT ABOUT ME?

EVY-IVY-OVER

P.S. WRITE SOON

A SUMMER'S WORTH OF SHAME

THE GATHERING ROOM

H, MY NAME IS HENLEY

KEEPING TIME

JULIE'S DAUGHTER

FITCHETT'S FOLLY

SYDNEY, HERSELF

Dog Days

COLBY RODOWSKY

Dog Days

PICTURES BY
KATHLEEN COLLINS HOWELL

Farrar, Straus and Giroux / New York

For my daughter-in-law, Julie.
And, of course, for Sandy and Mimi

Contents

Dog Days

– 1 –

The Not Very Good Summer

Rosie Riggs sat on the front steps and thought about summer. Her sister, Franny, sat beside her. Rosie wasn't sure what Franny was thinking, but she had a good idea because every few seconds Franny poked her in the ribs and said, "What'll we do *now*?" And each time she said it, the "now" got higher and higher and squeakier and squeakier.

"What'll we do *now*?" said Franny for what Rosie thought had to be the five hundredth time.
"Go play somewhere," said Rosie.
"Where?" said Franny.
"Anywhere," said Rosie.
"With you?" said Franny.
"No."
"Why not with you?"
"Because," said Rosie.
"Because why?" said Franny.

3

"Because I'm thinking," said Rosie.

"About what?" said Franny.

"About excruciatingly important matters," said Rosie.

"Oh," said Franny. She got up and went to the end of the walk, where she stood pulling leaves off the hedge and stuffing them down into the pockets of her shorts.

Rosie had just settled in to think when Franny was back, standing in front of her and saying, "What's 'ex-cru-ci-at-ing-ly'?"

"Very," said Rosie.

"Very what?"

"That's what it means. A lot of very," said Rosie.

"Oh," said Franny. And then, after a moment, "What very important matters?"

"Well," said Rosie, moving up a step and crossing her arms over her chest. "Like how this isn't going to be as good a summer as it would've been if Ann were here and not off in Minnesota." Ann was Rosie's best friend, who lived around the corner.

"Why is she?" said Franny. "In Minnesota."

"On account of her parents getting divorced and her father moving to Minnesota, and when it's his turn for Ann to be with him, that's where she has to go."

"Oh," said Franny again.

"*And*," said Rosie, getting back to why this wasn't

4

going to be as good a summer as it could have been. "How, starting now, Mom's going to be working in Aunt Kate's bookstore all year round and not just in the school year like she did before. *And* how just this morning, Lucy called and said she wasn't going to be able to baby-sit for us the way she said she would, on account of she got a chance to go to Cape Cod for the very whole summer, and she knew Mom would understand. Only Mom doesn't understand, and now she's in an excruciatingly bad mood and is calling everybody she can think of to see if they know anyone who wants to baby-sit."

"But Lucy promised," wailed Franny, sounding, thought Rosie, the way her mother sounded when she first heard the baby-sitter wasn't coming. "She promised to take us to the pool every day and to paint my fingernails and toenails with Pink Passion polish."

"Mine too," said Rosie. "Only now she's not. Only now she's changed her mind."

"I don't believe you and I'm going to ask Mom," shouted Franny, getting up and going inside and slamming the screen door behind her.

After Franny had gone, Rosie sat on the steps with her elbows on her knees and thought of one more reason why this wasn't going to be as good a summer as it could have been.

Franny.

"A whole summer of just me and Franny, with Ann gone and Mom not home to do stuff with, and now Lucy not even coming," said Rosie out loud. She got up and went down the steps and over to the hedge that separated the Riggses' house from the house next door, thinking how that was her only hope.

Even though Mr. and Mrs. Morgan had moved out just the day before, the house already had a deserted, forlorn look. The chairs were gone from the porch, and the gate to the back yard hung open. The curtainless windows were blank and staring, like eyes wearing sunglasses. For a minute, Rosie felt a lump of sadness growing inside of her. She thought about the Morgans—that as far back as she could remember, they had lived next door. She remembered how Mr. Morgan had let her plant a sunflower seed in the corner of his garden one summer, and how Mrs. Morgan had tried to teach the Riggses' dog, Mimi, to fetch.

The Morgans were nice and all, thought Rosie. But they weren't exactly people you could *play* with, what with their kids being even older than Mom and Dad. Rosie rubbed at her eyes, shook her head, and stood up straight. "But now they're gone," she said out loud. "And today or tomorrow or maybe next week, somebody new'll move in and"—she stopped to cross the fingers on both hands—"they *have* to have children."

Two, Rosie thought.

Two children. One for her, a girl who would be just Rosie's age and who would sleep in the room just opposite Rosie's room, and together they would form a secret club and call out the window to each other at night and early in the morning.

And another kid, thought Rosie. A girl, or maybe even a boy, who'd be the same age as Franny and tell "knock-knock" jokes and dig worms and do all the other dumb things Franny liked to do. And who'd play with Franny all day, every day, for the whole entire summer.

All of a sudden, Rosie felt a little nibble of worry in the back of her head. She remembered the night when Mrs. Morgan had come over to tell the Riggses that the house had been sold. "Are there children moving in?" Rosie had asked right out.

"Children?" said Mrs. Morgan, as if it were a word she hadn't heard before. "Well now, I don't know about that." She thought for a minute and then said, "But I declare, there must be." Her hands fluttered up like birds being let out of a cage. "I remember the realtor saying to Mr. Morgan that the new woman bought the house because of our big fenced back yard. And whoever they are, I know they'll be *very nice*."

Rosie wasn't too sure about that.

Mrs. Morgan thought everyone was *very nice*.

Even Skinny-bones Scott, whose real name was Destiny and who spoke in a whispery little voice and lived in the house at the corner with her aunt, Miss Flossie Scott.

Even Miss Flossie Scott herself, and the substitute mailman who left the mail on the corner of the porch, so it sometimes blew away or got wet by the rain.

And up until last year, Mrs. Morgan had even thought George Travis was *very nice*. That was before George had bombarded the Morgans' house with raw eggs one day when the temperature was ninety-eight degrees, and by the time Mr. Morgan tried to clean them off, the whole place smelled rotten, and sort of like throw-up.

"Besides," said Rosie to herself, "how could Mrs. Morgan *not* know whether there were children moving in when that's the first thing anybody *ought* to know. And how could she say that if there are, then she knows they'll be *very nice*, when they might *not* be. When they might be like Skinny-bones Scott, or George Travis. When they might be really abominable."

"Mom, what if they really are abominable?" called Rosie as her mother and Franny came out of the house.

"Who?"

"The kids who might move in next door."

"But, Rosie, we don't even know if there *are* children," said Mrs. Riggs, turning back to lock the door. "Now come along. I want to run over to the Tree House and pick up some books from Aunt Kate."

"There *have* to be," said Rosie. "Children, I mean."

"Well," said her mother, "I hope so for your sake."

"For mine, but mostly for Franny's," said Rosie, feeling, for a minute, the way she did in church when the organ was playing and the sun was streaming through the stained-glass windows. "So *she'll* have somebody to play with."

"That's lovely, Rosie."

"And not all the time be bugging me."

"Oh, Rosie," said her mother.

"What's 'a-bom-i-na-ble'?" said Franny.

"Like y—"

"Don't say it," cautioned Mrs. Riggs.

"Like liver," said Rosie. "Like liver and Brussels sprouts and George Travis rolled into one."

"Yuck," said Franny.

When they got out of the car, Mrs. Riggs and Franny went into the Tree House. Rosie stood for a minute looking up at Aunt Kate's store, which was in a row of other stores and not in a house at all, and definitely not in a tree. The Tree House was a children's bookstore and was filled, top to bottom, with picture books and paperbacks, fairy tales and fiction and non-fiction. There was a loft at one end, where Aunt Kate had her office, and a table under the stairs where real live authors sat when they came to the store to sign their books and talk to the children.

Rosie peered in the window, pretending to see the Tree House for the very first time. She saw Aunt Kate's cat sleeping on the counter and a huge stuffed Wild Thing sitting on a bench. She saw the posters and cutouts of book characters on the walls: Babar and Curious George, Madeline and Max.

Up until that spring there had even been a picture of Sandy the Super Dog, wearing a red bandanna around his neck and with his head raised, as if he was looking at something far away. When the edges of the poster had started to curl, Aunt Kate gave it to Rosie, who Scotch-taped it up over her bed at home. Sandy was the star of a whole series of books, including *Sandy's Baby-sitting Days, Sandy's Great Escape,* and *Sandy Saves the Day.* He was a large red golden retriever and was definitely Rosie's favorite book character. In fact, Sandy looked the way Rosie thought a dog *ought* to look and not at all like Mimi, who was small and black and scruffy and sometimes looked as if she ran on batteries.

Rosie watched her mother and Franny and Aunt Kate inside the store. After a while, she opened the door, setting the little bell overhead to jingling.

"Ah," said Aunt Kate, turning to look at her.

"Come on in, Rosie-posie. Your mother and I are just trying to think of a baby-sitter. And besides, I have a whole passel of new books to show you."

When they got home from the Tree House, Mrs. Riggs went back to the telephone. She called a friend of Aunt Kate's who had a teenage daughter, but the girl was already working at a candy store at the harbor, stirring fudge. She called Betsy and Melissa from the swimming pool, and Nancy from three blocks away, who sometimes came to baby-sit when Lucy was busy.

"Everybody who *wants* a job *has* a job," she said to Mr. Riggs when he came in from work late in the afternoon.

"We'll think of something," said Mr. Riggs, putting his arm around his wife and pulling her close.

"What?" said Mrs. Riggs. And Rosie thought her mother's voice sounded thin and wavery, the way it had the day the pipe burst in the upstairs bathroom and water was shooting every which way.

"How're we going to think of something?" said Mrs. Riggs. "When it's already the middle of June and I'm supposed to be at work on Wednesday and this is Monday and—"

"You could tell Aunt Kate you're not coming," said Rosie.

"Then I'd be no better than Lucy," said her mother. "Irresponsible, and feckless."

11

"What's 'feckless'?" said Franny.

"Like Lucy, I think," said Rosie.

"Besides," said their father, "your mother likes her job. It's important to her, and to all of us. Remember how we talked about that before. We'll have to find someone else."

"But not just anyone," said their mother. "That was the thing about Lucy. She liked the girls—and they liked her. And she was responsible. At least, I thought she was."

"Before we knew she was feckless," said Rosie.

That night for supper, the Riggses had corned beef hash out of a can, which was Rosie's least favorite meal. For dessert, they had Jell-O that Mrs. Riggs had made at the very last minute, and it spilled off the spoon instead of shaking *on* it, the way Jell-O was supposed to do. After they finished eating, Mr. Riggs got up to clear the table, saying, "Why don't you take Mimi and go for a walk, Joan. You need to get away from this telephone. Besides, if anyone calls, the girls and I can handle it."

Later, after the dishes were done and the kitchen was straight, Rosie was sitting on the porch swing listening to the story her father was telling about Mosey Bear in the palace of the Pharaoh when she heard her mother coming down the street. The slip-slap of Mrs. Riggs's sandals sounded quick and somehow excited as she turned into the walk and came up the steps.

"You'll never believe this," said Mrs. Riggs, "but I stopped and was talking to Miss Scott for the longest time. Didn't you see me up there? She was watering her flowers and—"

"They're plastic, and it is pretty unbelievable," said Mr. Riggs. "Plastic flowers and that fake plastic grass she has all over her front yard like a giant Astroturf doormat."

"Well, maybe she was washing them, then," said Mrs. Riggs. "But—"

"Like the time Mimi peed on them," said Rosie. "She had to wash them then, and she got really mad and called her a bad dog when how was *Mimi* supposed to know it was plastic."

"Well, Mimi didn't do anything *this* time, and Miss Scott called her 'nice doggie,' and anyway, everybody stop interrupting me—and guess what?"

"She knows someone who wants to baby-sit?" said Mr. Riggs.

"Better than that," said Mrs. Riggs, stepping back in a way that made Rosie think of a stage and the roll of drums.

"Better than that," Mrs. Riggs said again. *"She'll do it herself."*

"Who?" said Franny.

"Miss Scott," said her mother.

"Do what?" said Rosie.

"Take care of you girls."

"No," said Rosie, feeling suddenly that she was going to barf.

"Why on earth not?" said Mrs. Riggs.

"Sounds good to me," said Mr. Riggs.

"And to think she's been there all along," said Mrs. Riggs.

"She can't," said Rosie. And a thousand reasons swirled inside her head. Rosie caught hold of one of them and said, "On account of Skinny-bones. On account of Miss Scott having to stay home and take care of Skinny-bones Scott."

"No problem," said Mrs. Riggs, moving into the glow of the porch light. "Skinny-bones will be coming *with* her."

– 2 –

Miss Scott and
Skinny-bones Too

Rosie woke the next morning wondering how this had gone from being a not very good summer to the worst possible summer of her entire life. She remembered how happy and excited her mother had looked the night before when she told them Miss Flossie Scott was coming to baby-sit. She remembered how her mother had called Nana and Aunt Kate and even Granny Riggs in Cincinnati to tell them the news, and how Dad had taken them all out for ice cream cones afterward. And how, on the way home, Dad and Mom together had told them that this had all the earmarks of a really terrific summer.

"It has all the earmarks of a really *rotten* summer," Rosie said now. She looked up at the poster of Sandy the Super Dog over her bed, and for a minute she was sure he nodded in agreement. Then she reached under her bed and pulled out

16

the secondhand thesaurus Aunt Kate had gotten for her at a garage sale last year.

"Rotten," said Rosie, turning to the back of the book and running her finger down the page.

"Rotten," she said as she flipped to the center and made her way through a list of words. She sounded them out, a syllable at a time, then carefully copied something onto a piece of paper, tucking it into the pocket of her T-shirt as she got out of bed. She ran her tongue around the inside of her mouth, tasting the stale morning taste. She started down the steps, thinking that maybe she wouldn't brush her teeth ever again. Or bathe or get dressed, either one. "And probably I'll just waste away and then they'll be sorry—Franny and Dad and mostly Mom, on account of her being the one who fixed it for Miss Scott and awful old Skinny-bones to come. And when she asks me why I'm not dressed, that's what I'll tell her—that I'm wasting away," said Rosie under her breath as she headed for the kitchen.

But her mother didn't ask. Instead she smiled and waved her sponge and pointed to a bag of bagels on the table before she leaned back into the refrigerator, saying, "I want to get this cleaned out before Miss Scott comes tomorrow. I certainly don't want her to think we live with fuzzy green beans and dried-up broccoli stalks." Mrs. Riggs's voice sounded muffled as she went on. "Your father took the day off to help me get ready, but right now he's over at Hechingers trying to get a gizmo for that leaky faucet in the bathroom."

Rosie cleared her throat. "It doesn't matter about the refrigerator *or* the faucet in the bathroom, 'cause this is definitely going to be a *nefarious* summer," she said, patting the pocket of her T-shirt and hearing the piece of paper crackle.

"What's 'ne-far-i-ous'?" said Franny.

"Rotten. Sort of like 'abominable,' " said Rosie.

"Not exactly," said Mrs. Riggs. "I think 'nefarious' is different. More wicked, sort of."

"You're always saying how you want us to use new words," said Rosie. She eyed the bagels and wondered if wasting away meant not even eating a piece of one.

"I do," said Mrs. Riggs, as she finished cleaning the refrigerator and sat back on her heels. "I just want you to use them correctly. Anyway, summers aren't nefarious, people are."

"Nefarious. Miss Scott is nefarious," said Rosie.

"Is she? What Rosie said?" said Franny.

"Of course not," said Mrs. Riggs. "Miss Scott's lived here since before we moved into the neighborhood, and she's a lovely person. I mean, look at the way she took her great-niece Destiny in when the child's own mother couldn't raise her."

"Skinny-bones," said Rosie.

"Maybe we should all make an effort to call her by her real name," said Mrs. Riggs.

"Why?" said Rosie. "Nobody does, except maybe at school, and not always then, 'cause last year Mrs. Graham sometimes said, 'Skinny-bones, do this,' and sometimes, 'Destiny, do that.' And both ways the same person got up and did it.

"*Anyway,*" said Rosie, forgetting about the hungry feeling in the pit of her stomach; forgetting, even, about wasting away. "*Anyway,* you've majorly ruined my summer. We don't need Miss Scott, and we certainly don't need Skinny-bones, and why doesn't she stay home where she belongs, and I don't see why you just didn't get somebody *else.*"

Mrs. Riggs put the pitcher of orange juice, the milk, and the catsup back in the refrigerator. She put the lettuce in the crisper and the eggs in the rack on the inside of the door before she turned and faced her daughter. "Now look here, madame," she said. "You know we're in a bind. You know I tried everyone I could possibly think of. And you *know* I need a baby-sitter for you and Franny—"

"I'm not a baby."

"A caretaker, then. You know I need someone to take care of the two of you."

"I can take care of myself, and Franny, too," said Rosie.

Mrs. Riggs filled the ice trays and rubbed at the fingerprints on the outside of the door. "And," she went on, "when I was telling Miss Scott about my problem last night and she offered to come and help—I thought it was an answer to a prayer. And the fact that Skinny-bones'll be coming with her seems a definite plus. It'll give you girls a chance to get to know each other. And with Ann away, it'll be someone for you to hang around with."

"Mo-ther," said Rosie. "Why would I want to get to know Skinny-bones Scott? Why would I want to hang around her? Nobody hangs around Skinny-bones Scott.

"Skinny-bones Scott is a real loser. She wears pull-on pants instead of jeans, and hard shoes instead of sneakers. She wears blouses and not T-shirts and carries her books in a plastic K mart bag, and her socks creep down under her heels, and when we go on a class trip she always has to sit with somebody's *mother*. And the thing is she doesn't even mind. She doesn't even *know* it's queer to sit with somebody's *mother*."

"Will she take us to the pool?" asked Franny. "Miss Scott, I mean."

"To the pool?" said Rosie. "D'you really think Miss Scott's gonna take us to the *pool*? And anyway, why would you want her to? We'd have to take along a piece of real plastic grass so's she'd feel at home, and then she'd probably want to sit under a rain umbrella and not the regular beach kind, and then Skinny-bones'd come out with her dress bathing suit on her skinny-bones body, and people would know that we were together, and I'd expire right there in front of everybody."

"What's 'expire'?" said Franny.

"Die," said Rosie. "I'd die of embarrassment and humiliation and then you'd all be sorry.

"Wouldn't you?" she said into the silence that filled the room.

"Wouldn't you?" she said again, when nobody answered her.

Rosie looked at her father, who had come in and was standing just inside the kitchen door. She looked at Franny, at Mimi, at her mother. She waited for Mrs. Riggs to say her usual mother things about not caring how people looked or dressed or talked. And when she didn't, Rosie heard, from somewhere deep down inside of her, her own voice saying them to herself, almost as if she were taking a fill-in-the-blanks test at school.

"Well," said Mr. Riggs, after what Rosie thought was a very long time. "I guess Rosie has let us know how she feels. Which is all right. *However,* right now we've a bit of a problem, and what we're asking is that you girls give Miss Scott—and Skinny-bones—a chance. Okay?"

Rosie stood for a minute rubbing her foot against Mimi's back and wishing that the dog would come to her rescue: that she would growl or bark or do a trick, maybe even wet the floor—anything to get everyone to stop looking at *her.* Mimi sighed and settled deeper in sleep. And finally Rosie said, "Okay."

"Good," said Mr. Riggs in his "that's settled"

voice. "Now how about it—has everybody here had breakfast?"

"Not me," said Rosie. "And I guess I'm hungry."

"Maybe she won't come," said Rosie as she sat on her mother's bed the next morning and watched her get ready for work.

"Who?" said Mrs. Riggs.

"Miss Scott," said Rosie. "Maybe she had to go to the dentist, or to California. Maybe she changed her mind."

"She'll come. She said she would," said Mrs. Riggs.

"So'd Lucy. Maybe Miss Scott is feckless the way Lucy was feckless." Rosie slid her tongue around the word, liking the way it sounded.

"I don't think so," said her mother. "Besides, it's almost time for her to be here."

"Maybe she'll have had a body transplant and all of a sudden've turned into Mary Poppins and wear funny shoes and carry an umbrella with a parrot's head on the handle and a carpetbag filled with more than it can ever hold. Maybe she'll be magic, sort of, and arrive on the end of a kite string and not be half as bad as I know she'll be. And maybe she won't bring Skinny-bones."

"Maybe," said Mrs. Riggs in a way that let Rosie know she wasn't really listening. She leaned close to the mirror to put her earrings in and said, "I

23

hear Mimi barking. Look and see if Miss Scott's coming now."

Rosie slid off the bed and went over to the window. She knelt on the floor with her chin on the windowsill, her eyes closed. She felt afraid and excited, both at the same time, to see who was coming down the street.

But Miss Scott had not turned into Mary Poppins. She didn't come at the end of a kite string but on her own two feet, in galoshes, carrying an umbrella with the spokes sticking out and a tote bag with a smiley face on the side. She walked quickly, stepping over puddles and calling over her shoulder for Skinny-bones to hurry up. Skinny-bones held her K mart bag on her head and walked backwards with her tongue out to catch the rain.

Rosie watched as they turned onto the walk. She put her hands up to her neck, rolled her eyes, and made gagging noises deep inside her throat. "I have a serious illness. Maybe fatal," she said as she slumped onto the floor.

"I wish you a speedy recovery, then," said her mother as she picked up her shoulder bag off the dresser. She leaned over and tousled her daughter's red hair before she went out of the bedroom.

Rosie waited for a minute, on the floor next to the window in her mother's room, hoping that Miss Scott had come to say that she couldn't stay; that

she had changed her mind about baby-sitting; that she had too much to do at home to be able to take care of Rosie and Franny Riggs. That she was, indeed, feckless.

She went out into the hall, sat on the top step, and listened as her mother opened the door for Miss Scott and Skinny-bones. She slid on her backside halfway down the steps, peering through the balusters and listening as her mother asked Skinny-bones about her vacation and talked about the weather.

"I'm certainly glad to see this rain," said Mrs. Riggs. "It'll make the flowers grow." Rosie saw her mother put her hand over her mouth just as Miss Scott's laugh broke out and filled the corners of the room.

"Ho-ho-ho," laughed Miss Scott, rocking back on her heels and slapping the side of her leg. "Ho-ho-ho. Not mine it won't. It won't make *my* flowers grow."

"That's on account of they're plastic," said Franny, pushing in between her mother and Miss Scott. "Why *are* they?"

"Old bones," said Miss Scott. "Old bones and the fact that stooping and squatting aren't as easy as they once were. So I went to the dime store and got me some plastic flowers, and now I'm all set."

"Old bones, old bones, old bones," sang Franny.

"Old bones, old bones, old *tired* bones," sang Miss Flossie Scott in return.

"Well, yes," said Mrs. Riggs. "Now let me show you around. Here's the television—though we don't have cable, but if there's anything you want to watch on one of the regular channels, feel free."

She never lets us watch during the day, thought Rosie as she came the rest of the way down the stairs and leaned around the newel post, trying to give her mother the evil eye. But Mrs. Riggs had moved on and was heading for the kitchen with Miss Scott, Franny, and Skinny-bones following her. Rosie waited a minute and then trailed along behind.

"Here's the phone—and there's a list of emergency numbers on the inside of the cupboard door. There's coffee on the stove, and I'm sure you can find something in the fridge for lunch."

"Ha," said Rosie to herself. "As if she hadn't gone out to the deli last night and come home with ham and turkey and three kinds of cheese like maybe we were having the Queen of England for lunch and not just dumb old Miss Scott and Skinny-bones."

Mrs. Riggs swung around to face her, and for a minute Rosie was afraid she'd spoken out loud. "Why, here's Rosie," her mother said. "You know Miss Scott and Destiny, don't you?"

"Yes," said Rosie. She rubbed at a spot on the floor with the toe of her tennis shoe.

"I'll be on my way now," said Mrs. Riggs. She turned toward the door, then stopped, looking back, and saying, in a voice that Rosie thought was just for her, "Have fun today."

After her mother had left for work, Rosie stood at the kitchen door and watched the rain. She watched it splash against the steps and run along the driveway and make puddles in the yard. She watched it beat against the rose bushes and the hedge and the empty house next door.

"What'll we do *now?*" she heard Franny say in back of her. "What'll we do *now?*"

Rosie turned slowly, thinking that she would tell Franny to get her Chutes and Ladders game, or lotto, or even pick up sticks. That maybe they would play. But just then she saw Miss Scott reach into her tote bag and take out a box, give it a shake, and spill what was inside out onto the table in front of Franny.

"Buttons," she said.

"Buttons?" said Franny.

"Well, indeed, buttons," said Miss Scott. "You can string them, or stack them, or sort them out. You can spin them or hide them or . . ."

Rosie walked out of the kitchen and through the dining room. She went into the living room, stepping over Skinny-bones, who lay on her stomach, on the floor, with her feet up in the air, reading a book. She opened the front door and felt the rain as it blew across the porch and onto her face. She closed the door and sighed.

In the afternoon, the sun came out and the sidewalk steamed and finally dried. Miss Scott sat on the porch swing sewing tufts of new red wool hair on Franny's Raggedy Ann doll. Franny sat beside her, wearing her button necklace and singing the "Old bones, old bones, old tired bones" song.

Out on the driveway, Skinny-bones drew a hopscotch court with yellow chalk. She took a rubber heel out of her pocket and dropped it onto number one. She hopped and balanced and threw the heel again, moving on through two and three and four and five.

Rosie sat on the front steps and waited for Skinny-bones to miss. "Then it'll be my turn," she said to herself. "Skinny-bones'll ask—or I'll just say it is. And I'll show *her*. I'll go on out there, and it won't matter that I've never played dumb old hopscotch before. I'll hop and jump and spin around without once teetering or falling sideways or touching the ground, and when I'm done, then everybody up and down the street, and maybe around the corner, will open their doors and come out on their porches and yell and cheer and—"

But Skinny-bones went on, through six and seven and eight and nine and *ten*.

And when she was finished, she stood for a minute tossing the rubber heel up in the air and catching it again.

Rosie sat pushing at paint blisters on the underside of the steps and listening to the squeak of the swing. Then she got up and went upstairs and flopped down on her bed. "This has *got* to be the longest day of the longest week of the longest month of the longest summer that ever was," said Rosie to the poster of Sandy on the wall. But for once Sandy seemed to be looking the other way.

When her mother came in from work, Rosie heard Franny telling her all the things they had done that day. She heard her telling about buttons and new hair for Raggedy Ann and about sandwiches cut from corner to corner instead of straight down the middle. After a while, Mrs. Riggs came upstairs. She stopped at the door of Rosie's room, saying, "Well, Rosie-posie, how was it?"

"Abominable," said Rosie. "And nefarious, too."

– 3 –

Moving Day

The next morning, Franny and Miss Scott made snakes out of Play-Doh at the kitchen table. They told "knock-knock" jokes and watched a worm slither across the driveway.

Out on the front porch, Rosie lay on the swing, pushing it back and forth with one foot and watching the shadows on the ceiling. Skinny-bones Scott sat on the top step, reading a book.

All of a sudden George Travis screeched around the corner on his bike. He rode across the grass and tore at shrubs. He bounced over the curb, splattering bits of gravel and pulling his bike up onto the back wheel and hanging there, as if he were breaking a bucking bronco.

"Hey, ugly," he said, bringing his bike down hard on the front wheel. "Hey, ugly bean pole, what're you doing here? Why aren't you up at your end of the block?"

" 'Cause she's with me, that's why," called Rosie, moving over to sit on the step.

"Arrrgh. Two uglies. A bean pole and a carrot top." He spun away, circling around as he chanted, "Fire, fire, head's on fire."

"I *hate* it when he says that," said Rosie.

"I *hate* it when he calls me bean pole," said Skinny-bones.

"It's not *my* fault I have red hair."

"It's not *my* fault I'm skinny."

"D'you hate 'Skinny-bones,' then? Being called it, I mean?" said Rosie.

"That's my *name*, but I never heard *anybody* called Bean Pole."

George sailed down the street with his arms straight out. He caught the handlebars at the last minute, jumped the curb, and turned into the Riggs walkway.

"You better not. This's private property," shouted Rosie.

"Says who? Anyway, it's a free country."

"Get off our sidewalk, George."

"You gonna make me? Huh, Carrot Top?"

"Hush," said Skinny-bones, sliding closer on the step and poking Rosie in the ribs. "Aunt Flossie says to just act like he's not here," she hissed.

"But he *is* here," said Rosie.

"Make like you don't see him," said Skinny-bones.

"I *do* see him, though."

33

"Pretend we're having a conversation."

"About what?"

"It doesn't have to be *about* anything, so long as he thinks we're talking and not paying any mind to him."

Rosie thought for a minute. Then, keeping her voice as low as Skinny-bones's, she said, "New people're moving in next door, and they're maybe gonna have a girl just my age who'll be my second-best best friend, after Ann."

"Louder," said George, inching his bike down the walk.

"I have this book," whispered Skinny-bones. "It's about a dog, and you could read it when I'm done. It's from the library, but there's ages left before it's due."

"I have about a ton of books," said Rosie. "Maybe a million. On account of my aunt running a bookstore."

"I'm talking to you, Uglies," said George.

"What kind of books?" said Skinny-bones.

"All kinds," said Rosie. "I even have a thesaurus that tells me a bunch of words that mean the same as other words. Aunt Kate got it secondhand, and that's where I found out about nefarious. George Travis is nefarious."

"Yeah, rotten," said Skinny-bones.

"More like wicked, my mother says."

"Yeah, wicked George Travis is nefarious," said Skinny-bones.

"I am not," said George, ramming the front wheel of his bike into the steps.

"Nefarious George," said Rosie, leaning over to whisper in Skinny-bones's ear.

"Say what, Carrot Top?" shouted George, backing his bike up and running into the steps again. "Say what? Anyway, I'm out of here, but you'd better watch it, 'cause I'll be back. And when I am, then you'll be sorry."

"Nefarious George," exploded Rosie and Skinny-bones both at the same time. "Nefarious George. Ne-far-i-ous George." They rocked backwards and forwards, laughing and choking and coughing as tears rolled down their faces.

"And when I am—*beware*," called George as he spun his bike around and shot up the walk. He clipped the hedge and bumped down the curb. He stopped and started and left tire marks all the way up the street and around the corner.

Rosie flopped back onto the porch. She looked at the ceiling and thought how her ribs hurt from laughing and how it was a good kind of hurting. Skinny-bones flopped back next to her.

"Do you think he will?" said Skinny-bones.

"Come back?"

"Yeah."

"Yeah. On account of he's on our street more than he's on his own. But who cares? Who's afraid of Nefarious George with his sticking-up hair and his gross old gray sweat suit . . ."

"Even in summer . . ."

"And that's got to stink to high heaven," said Rosie. She stopped and sat up, feeling all of a sudden the way she had the time her father was teaching her to ride a two-wheel bike and let go, leaving Rosie to ride alone. I'm talking to her, she thought. I—Rosie Rosemary Ann Riggs—am talking to Skinny-bones Destiny Scott.

Rosie sat for a minute, wondering what to do. She listened to the silence all around her. She sighed, and shrugged, and after a while she went on, "It's weird, kind of, the way all summer long, or at least since school was out, Franny's been saying 'What'll we do *now*'—and all of a sudden she has stuff to do and I don't."

"Yeah," said Skinny-bones, sitting up beside her. "Same as it's weird for me to have to be here and not at my house, where I'd rather be."

"How come?" said Rosie.

"Because of Aunt Flossie. Because she said your mother was in a pretty pickle on account of the baby-sitter—"

"Lucy. She's feckless."

"On account of Lucy not coming and how it was the neighborly thing for us to do to help her out. And besides, she's getting paid for it."

"Not how come *that*, how come you'd rather be at your house?" Rosie looked up the street at the little yellow house with the window shades all in a row and the plastic grass shining in the sunlight.

"Because I'm not company there," said Skinny-bones in her whispery voice.

"Are you company here?" said Rosie.

"I don't *live* here, and if you don't live someplace, then you're company."

"I guess," said Rosie. She thought for a minute of all the bad things about being company: how you had to ask every time you wanted a drink of water and have to worry when you flushed the toilet that maybe it might overflow, or else that the door would stick and you'd have to stay in a strange bathroom forever.

Rosie was trying to decide whether or not to tell Skinny-bones, if the Riggses' bathroom door stuck, to kick it once on the bottom and push down on the handle, when she heard the truck. It rumbled and roared and lumbered down the street, turning around at the corner and coming back to stop in front of the house next door. It was large and green, with EASY MOVING on the side in white letters, and seemed to take up all the street; to make the houses, the trees, the cars, look small and fragile, as if they belonged in a Christmas garden.

Rosie and Skinny-bones got up and went down the walk. They stood at the hedge and listened as the truck shuddered and sputtered and was finally quiet. They watched as the men jumped out, threw open the big side door, and put down the ramp. They saw a yellow Volkswagen bug pull up behind the truck and a woman and a dog get out.

"I don't see any girl," said Skinny-bones. "I don't see any second-best best friend."

"She's coming later," said Rosie. "She's with her father, and maybe her brothers and sisters. And they stopped at McDonald's for egg McMuffins. Or maybe at the store."

George Travis rode down the sidewalk, cutting in front of the truck and out into the street. When he came around the second time, he shouted, "Remember, Uglies. I'll be back . . ."

The woman from the yellow Volkswagen went up the steps of the Morgans' old house. She unlocked the door and took the dog inside, but in a minute she was back, standing at the curb and talking to the movers.

"She doesn't look like she's anybody's mother. I mean, not anybody *our* age," said Skinny-bones.

Rosie stared hard at the woman. She was short and shaped like a sofa cushion. She had scraggly gray hair piled up on her head, and when she talked, her arms seemed to spin, like the arms of a windmill. As Rosie watched, she picked up an umbrella stand, beckoned to the movers, and led the way into the house.

"She's the aunt, then, or the granny," said Rosie. "They probably come from somewhere far away, and the rest of the family's back at the motel and they'll be along after a while."

"Maybe," said Skinny-bones. "And maybe not. Maybe that's all there is—that lady and that dog."

"No," said Rosie, and her fingers ached from clenching them into fists.

Franny ran out of the house, slamming the screen door behind her. "Are they here yet? Are the new people here?" she said, dancing down the steps. "We heard the truck, and Miss Scott said I could watch but to stay out of the way. To not be a pest. Did you see them?"

"Only the granny," said Rosie.

"Who might be the lady of the house," said Skinny-bones.

"Who might not," said Rosie.

"Come on," said Franny. "Let's get closer. I want to *see*."

Rosie and Franny and Skinny-bones Scott moved up the sidewalk next to the truck. They watched the movers carry a bed and a washer and a kitchen table into the house next door. They watched them carry a sofa and chairs and a little organ; pictures in frames, lamps, mirrors, and a lot of brown cardboard boxes that all looked the same.

But where's the swing set? thought Rosie. Where're the bikes and the sled and the pogo stick? Where're the Barbie dolls and the stuffed animals and the girl's bed with the canopy over the top?

"Where's the kid stuff?" asked Skinny-bones, and for a minute Rosie thought she had read her mind.

"In the truck," said Rosie. "First what they do is to get everything all set up and then they'll bring it out. The swing set and the bikes and the pogo stick."

"You could ask," said Skinny-bones. "You could go right up to that mover with the yellow mustache and ask him if there're any kids."

"No," said Rosie, who all of a sudden didn't want to know if there wasn't any girl moving into the house next door. Any second-best best friend.

"*I* will," said Franny. And before Rosie could stop her, Franny was running after one of the movers as he balanced a chest of drawers on his back and made his way up the walk. She saw him stop and stand there, swaying, as he said something to Franny. She saw her sister turn and run back.

"I did it," said Franny. "I asked him were there any children, and he said he didn't think so. He said there was that lady, and she was a writer, and that every one of those boxes is full of books, and how they have to carry them all inside, and why didn't I just run along."

Rosie and Skinny-bones sat on the back steps eating their peanut butter and jelly sandwiches. They felt the sun beating down on their heads and listened to George Travis making Tarzan yells as he rode his bike on the street out front. They listened to the movers going thumpity thump as they went up and down the ramp to the truck, carrying more cardboard boxes of books.

"At least maybe Mimi'll be happy," said Skinnybones. "Maybe she and that new dog'll be friends. Maybe real best friends and not even second-best."

"Yeah," said Rosie, "except that sometimes Mimi's sort of boring. I mean mostly she just sleeps and snorts and scratches and hardly notices things she's supposed to notice. And she *never* does anything splendiferous."

Just then the new woman opened the back door and let the dog out into the yard. Rosie and Skinnybones watched through the fence as the dog sniffed the hydrangea bush. They watched him dig a hole next to the birdbath and go to the bathroom on Mrs. Morgan's hollyhocks. After a while he trotted over to the fence, standing on his hind legs and putting his front paws on the top. His red bandanna rippled, like a flag, in the breeze.

"That's a golden retriever," said Rosie.

"Yeah," said Skinny-bones. "And he looks sort of—"

"Familiar," said Rosie.

"Like when you see somebody—"

"And know maybe you've seen that somebody someplace before—"

"But you can't think where. Except I think I can.

43

Come on." Skinny-bones jumped up, pulling Rosie behind her. They went through the kitchen and the dining room and into the living room, where Skinny-bones reached into her K mart bag and pulled out a book. "Here—the book I was telling you about. It's my all-time favorite and I keep getting it from the library. It's about this dog—"

"Named Sandy," said Rosie, reaching out to touch the cover of the book. "It's mine too, only this is *Sandy the Super Dog*, and my absolutely positively favorite is *Sandy's Great Adventure*—you know, the one where Sandy rescues this kid in the woods and—"

"Yeah, but look," said Skinny-bones, turning to the inside back flap and pointing to a black-and-white photograph of a dog. "It says, 'Sandy, a golden retriever, belongs to author Dawn O'Day, who has written many exciting stories about him.' "

"Come upstairs," said Rosie, leading the way up the steps. She ran into her room, stopped in front of the poster, and threw out her arms. "Ta-dum . . ." she said. "Introducing Sandy the Super Dog."

"Sandy," whispered Skinny-bones.

"That's on account of he was in Aunt Kate's bookstore, and the edges were crumpling, but I didn't care. I just used more Scotch tape."

Rosie ran and got the binoculars out of her father's closet and brought them back. She held them up to her eyes and looked out at the yard next door. Then she handed them to Skinny-bones.

"The bandanna's the same," she said.

"And the ears," said Skinny-bones.

"That feathery kind of hair on the legs."

"And the way he's sitting there, with one paw sort of up, like on the cover of *Sandy's Baby-sitting Days*."

"It might be," said Rosie.

"D'you think?"

"Maybe."

"It could be."

"Cross your fingers."

"I *hope*."

"And hold your breath."

Just then Franny came to the door. She stood for a minute, watching the two older girls, before moving up beside them. "What're you doing?" she said.

"Looking at the new neighbor," said Skinny-bones.

"At Sandy the Super Dog," said Rosie.

"He's awesome," said Skinny-bones.

"And splendiferous," said Rosie.

"What's 'splen-dif-er-ous'?" said Franny.

"Good," said Rosie. "Only better. More like wonderful."

"Yeah," said Skinny-bones Scott.

– 4 –

Introducing Sandy
the Super Dog

When Rosie called the Tree House, her mother answered the phone. "Mom," said Rosie. "It's positively splendiferous."

"What?" said Mrs. Riggs.

"Not what—who," said Rosie.

"Who, then?"

"Sandy the Super Dog."

"Well, yes," said Mrs. Riggs. "I guess he is. But why are you calling me at work to tell me this? I mean, why, all of a sudden?"

"Because he's *here*."

"Who?"

"Sandy."

"Where?"

"Mom, aren't you *listening*? Here. Next door, I mean."

"Ro-sie. What *are* you talking about?" said Mrs. Riggs.

"The new people moved in next door, only it's not people exactly but only this woman, and she has this dog, and Skinny-bones and I've been watching, and it's *Sandy*. We know it is."

"You and Skinny-bones? Skinny-bones Scott?"

"Me and Skinny-bones."

"Skinny-bones and *I*," reminded Mrs. Riggs.

"Skinny-bones and I," said Rosie. "Anyway, this lady moved in and she's a writer—the mover told us so—and she has this dog, and Skinny-bones and I just know it's Sandy."

"Don't be silly, Rosie," said Mrs. Riggs.

"And he looks just like my poster," said Rosie before her mother had a chance to say any more. "And like the picture on the flap of the book jacket where it says, 'Sandy, a golden retriever, belongs to author Dawn O'Day, who has written many exciting stories about him.'"

"But, Rosie," her mother went on. "Dawn O'Day lives in Smithfield, Virginia. I know because Aunt Kate wrote to her, to see if she could get her to come to the Tree House for an autographing. She wrote back and said she doesn't *do* autographings. She doesn't *do* speeches. She doesn't *do* anything."

"She writes books," said Rosie. "Anyway, Mom, listen. He's wearing a red bandanna."

"So do lots of dogs," said Mrs. Riggs.

"And he's a *golden retriever*."

"All golden retrievers look alike."

"Mom—I can't believe you said that. That's like saying that all Chinese people look alike. Or all black people. And you always said that was an abominable thing to say."

"It *is* an abominable thing to say, and I'm sorry," said Mrs. Riggs. "But right now I have to go. The store's crowded and there're people waiting for me to help them. I'll talk to you later."

"Mothers," said Rosie, hanging up the phone and turning to Skinny-bones. "Can you believe what she just said?"

"That all golden retrievers look alike?"

"Yeah," said Rosie.

"That's better than what Aunt Flossie said," said Skinny-bones. "When I went down and told her that Sandy had moved in next door to you and across the street from us, do you know what she said? She said, *'Who's Sandy?'* That's like saying, 'Who's Elvis?' "

"Or who's E.T.?"

"Who's George Washington?"

"Mothers *and* aunts," said Rosie.

"Yeah," said Skinny-bones.

Rosie watched through the binoculars as the dog next door settled into a patch of sunlight. "Just think," she said. "With Sandy the Super Dog right next door, we can watch him every day, all summer long."

48

"And get to know him."

"Maybe take him for walks."

"Go *with* him on his adventures."

"Right now he looks sort of tired, though," said Rosie, handing the binoculars to Skinny-bones. "Like maybe all that moving really got to him."

"Either that, or he just finished some wonderful kind of daring deed."

"Something splendiferous, and he has to rest."

"Like when Sandy was kidnapped by the jewel thieves and taken far away and had to get loose and make his way home," said Skinny-bones.

"And swam across the river, against the current," said Rosie.

"And braved thunder and lightning . . ."

"Went down the side of the mountain, and into the cave . . ."

"In all that dark—with all those bats."

"And when he got home *that* time, he was so tired he went right to sleep, before he had his kibble."

"Or even a biscuit."

The girls watched for a minute as the dog got up and moved out of the sun and into the shade of a forsythia bush. "We could call him and see if he answers," said Skinny-bones. And together they pushed up the screen and leaned out the window, resting their elbows on the sill.

"Hey, Sandy," called Rosie. The dog looked up and thumped his tail on the ground.

"What're you doing?" said Franny from the side yard, where she was digging for worms.

"Calling the dog, obviously," said Rosie. "And he answered, too. Wagging his tail is the way a dog answers—in case you didn't *know*."

"I know that," said Franny. "I know as much about dogs as *you* do. Hey, Sandy," said Franny, moving closer to the fence. The dog thumped his tail again.

"Hey, Brownie . . .

"Hey, Dog . . .

"Hey, Rover . . ." called Franny. And each time she called a name, the dog in the yard next door looked up and wagged his tail.

"See," said Franny, turning and yelling up to the window. "He answers to everything. I bet that's just any old dog and not Sandy at all. I bet his name is Prince or Rex or Fred, and that he's not somebody splen-dif-er-ous like you said."

"He is too," said Rosie. "That's the world-famous Sandy the Super Dog—it's just that probably he's traveling incognito."

"What's 'in-cog-ni-to'?" said Franny.

"In disguise," said Skinny-bones.

The girls waited until Franny had packed up her worm-digging equipment and disappeared around front before they went downstairs and out into the back yard. "See, he's got tags on his collar, and I'll bet anything they tell his name and his owner's name and where he lives, stuff like that," said Rosie, going to stand beside the fence. "And all we have to do is call him over and read them, and then we'll know. I mean we know now, but then we'll *know* know. For sure, I mean."

"Yeah," said Skinny-bones, moving up next to her. "But I already feel it in my bones, the way Aunt Flossie can feel a storm coming up in her knees, or sometimes her toes."

"So go ahead, read the tags," said Rosie.

"No, you," said Skinny-bones.

"How come?"

" 'Cause it's your idea—and your yard."

"Yeah," said Rosie. "But I'll let you, because you're company. That's one good thing about being company."

"The writer lady might see us," said Skinny-bones.

"She might," said Rosie. "Unless she's inside unpacking all those nine thousand boxes of books. Or making the bed, or rice pudding."

"Besides," said Skinny-bones, "don't you think, if you had this really important dog, that you'd have a bodyguard for it. Or the secret service. Hiding somewhere, I mean."

"Or an excruciatingly loud burglar alarm," said Rosie. "And if we even leaned one inch over that fence or reached for Sandy's tags, a bell would ring and the police would come. And maybe even the FBI."

The girls backed slowly away from the fence. "We'll wait awhile," said Rosie.

"And watch," said Skinny-bones.

"And see what happens."

When the movers had finished unloading the truck, they pulled in the ramp and slammed the doors. The driver revved up the engine, and the truck lumbered down the street and around the corner, leaving the neighborhood suddenly quiet. Rosie and Skinny-bones dawdled in the back yard, watching the dog next door and wishing that he would wake up, that he would come over to the fence, that somehow they could learn his name. They set up the Scrabble game on the back porch and Rosie made the word XRAY. Skinny-bones crossed it with the word ZEBRA, then Rosie added the word ZIP along the top.

"Can I play?" said Franny, coming around the side of the house and up the steps.

"No," said Rosie.

"Why not?" said Franny.

" 'Cause you don't know any words," said Rosie.

"I do too. I know 'in-cog-ni-to.' You just said it a while back."

"You can't spell it, though," said Rosie.

"So what?" said Franny. "I can *say* it, and besides I didn't want to play anyway, 'cause Miss Scott and I're gonna make lemonade out of real lemons and not a can. And *you* can't have any."

53

As Franny opened the door to go inside, Mimi pushed her way out, skittering over the Scrabble board and sending tiles across the porch and onto the grass below. She flew down the steps and over to the fence, pushing against it with her nose and barking her shrill yappy bark. In the yard next door, the golden retriever got up. He ran to his side of the fence, planted his legs, with his rump up in the air, wagged his tail, and barked a deep rolling bark. And then they were off: racing the length of the fence, sliding, skidding, and kicking up clumps of earth; turning at the end of the yard to come back the other way. Up and down. Up and down.

Suddenly the new woman opened her back door and whistled. The golden retriever stopped and stood for a minute, as if thinking about what to do next. Then he turned and trotted across the yard and into the house.

"D'you see that?" said Rosie. "The way he ran across the yard with his head up."

"And his tail straight out in back," said Skinny-bones.

"Like he was someone famous."

"And used to being on book jackets."

"A real celebrity."

"And maybe even in the newspapers."

"Not like *some* dogs I know," said Rosie, looking down at Mimi, who had finally stopped racing along the fence and had collapsed on the grass, snorting and panting and gasping for breath.

When Mrs. Riggs came home from work, she brought cookies from the bakery. "These are for us," she said, handing a white paper bag to Franny without even telling her to save them for after supper. "The ones in the *box* are for Dawn O'Day."

"Dawn O'Day?" shrieked Rosie. "But you said Dawn O'Day lived in Virginia. You said not to be silly, and that all golden retrievers looked alike."

"I know what I said, and I was wrong; at least, *maybe* I was wrong," said her mother. "After you called, Aunt Kate telephoned the sales rep from Miss O'Day's publisher and asked if she was moving to Baltimore, and he said yes—he didn't know exactly where, but she was moving here to be closer to her brother and his family."

"I told you," said Rosie. "And if that's Dawn O'Day, then *he*—the dog—really is *Sandy.*"

"Except that he's in-cog-ni-to," said Franny.

"Incognito?" said Mrs. Riggs.

"Yeah, we told her that," said Rosie, "on account of she said he wasn't really Sandy. That he was probably Prince or Rex—"

"Or Fred," said Skinny-bones.

"Oh, I see," said Mrs. Riggs. "Well, I guess it's *possible* for dogs to be incognito, though I've never heard of it. Mostly people are, I think."

Just then Aunt Kate knocked on the screen door and came inside. "I got here as soon as I could, after I closed the store," she said. "Have you gone over yet? Is it really Miss O'Day? What did she say?"

"You're going over *there*?" asked Rosie. "To Sandy's house?"

"Yes. Kate and I thought that it would be nice if I were to take a little gift, sort of to welcome the new woman to the neighborhood."

"Then afterward," said Aunt Kate, "if it *is* Dawn O'Day, we can all get to meet her *and* Sandy. And I can try to convince them both to come to the Tree House for a visit."

Aunt Kate, Rosie, Skinny-bones, Franny, and even Miss Scott crowded out onto the porch and watched as Mrs. Riggs went along the sidewalk, across the lawn, and up the steps of the house next door. They listened as she knocked on the door, and they leaned forward and held their breath, waiting for someone to answer it.

In a few minutes, Mrs. Riggs was back looking red in the face, as if it were hotter than it actually was.

"What'd you say?" asked Aunt Kate.

"I said, 'Hi, I'm Joan Riggs, and I just wanted to drop these cookies off to welcome you to the neighborhood.' "

"What'd *she* say?" said Rosie.

"She said, 'I'm Dawn O'Day,' and 'Thank you.'

And then," Mrs. Riggs went on, "before I had a chance to say, 'Dawn O'Day, the writer?' or 'That must be Sandy, then,' she said, 'Thank you' again, and closed the door."

"Oh," said Aunt Kate.

"Oh," said Rosie and Skinny-bones.

"Oh," said Franny.

"Fiddle-faddle," said Miss Scott.

Later that night, after Rosie had reread the last four chapters of *Sandy's Baby-sitting Days*, she turned out the light and sat at her window looking over at the house next door. In the room opposite hers, where the second-best best friend was supposed to be, the lights were on and the shades were up. Rosie watched as Dawn O'Day unpacked a box of books, blowing at each one and putting it on the shelf. She saw Sandy wander into the room and climb up onto a couch, settling down with his head on his paws.

After a while, Rosie got up and went over to the bed. She slid the book under her pillow and looked up at the poster. She thought of the dog sleeping on the couch next door. She closed her eyes and saw the window of Aunt Kate's store, all filled with copies of a brand-new book. There was a dog on the cover, and a girl with curly red hair. And across the top of every book jacket, in letters that seemed to grow and grow and grow, was the title: *Sandy and Rosie Riggs*.

− 5 −

The Fair

"The thing is," said Rosie to Skinny-bones as they sat under the hydrangea bushes, feeling the cool, flat dirt with their bare feet and watching the sunlight through the leaves. "The thing is—here we are right next door to Sandy the Super Dog, and we might as well not be. We might as well be next to the Morgans who used to live there, or Miss Cook on the other side."

"Or the Corellis across the street," said Skinny-bones.

"*And*," Rosie went on, "the very day after Sandy and Miss O'Day moved in, I wrote a letter to Ann in Minnesota telling her all about it and saying that I'd write again with the next installment—only there isn't any next installment. And it's been a week."

"That's 'cause nothing's happened," said Skinny-bones.

"It's abominable," said Rosie.

"And boring, too," said Skinny-bones.

"On account of what Sandy mostly does is sleep. Outside in the sun, or in the hole he dug in that thing that used to be a fishpond, only Mr. Morgan filled it in with dirt, so now it's a flower bed."

"And Miss O'Day sits upstairs in that room opposite yours and types in stops and starts, and times when she stops I just hold my breath waiting for her to start up again." Skinny-bones leaned back against the side of the house, pulled up her pointy knees, and tapped on them, as if they were a typewriter: *Tap-tap-tap* Pause *Tap-tap-tap-tap-tap* Pause *Tap* Pause *Tap*

"Only what I don't understand is how she has anything to type *about* when Sandy doesn't *do* anything."

"He does too," said Rosie. "Sandy does *everything*. It's just that I think he already *did* it. Before, sometime. Maybe last month, or a long time ago."

"How come you think that?"

"On account of this author who came to the Tree House once. She explained how when a writer writes a book, she ends up using a whole bunch of things that have happened in her life—and some that haven't—and sometimes she doesn't know she's going to use them and they just pop up there, like mushrooms after a spring rain."

"That's what she said? Like mushrooms?" said Skinny-bones.

"Yeah," said Rosie.

61

"After a spring rain?"

"Yeah."

"Weird," said Skinny-bones. She thought for a minute before she said, "You mean that some of the things that've happened this week might end up in a Sandy book? Like the moving truck coming and unloading all those books, and George Travis doing wheelies in the street. Like the time your aunt Kate came and waited around until Miss O'Day went outside, and then she ran over and asked if she and Sandy would come to the bookstore, and Miss O'Day said no. Or when we sat underneath her workroom window and talked about our favorite parts in the books in our loudest-ever voices and hoped that Miss O'Day would ask us in—but she didn't."

Skinny-bones picked up two boxes of apple juice and handed one to Rosie. She poked the straw down into her drink, took a swallow, and said, "Do you think *we* could ever be in a Sandy book? You and me, because of us living here and Miss O'Day seeing us, whether she wants to or not? And maybe we'll be like mushrooms in her mind, and when she's typing one day, she'll just put us in, along with the jewel thieves, and the kids Sandy baby-sat for, and all the rest. Do you think?"

Rosie closed her eyes and saw the brand-new book: the one that said *Sandy and Rosie Riggs* on the cover.

She opened her eyes and saw Skinny-bones leaning close and grinning like a jack-o'-lantern.

She closed her eyes and saw the book again. She saw the dog on the cover, and the person with red curly hair, and there, way in the back, a string bean of a girl. She saw a new title that said: *Sandy and Rosie Riggs (and Skinny-bones).*

"Maybe," said Rosie. "Just maybe. But that's all the more reason why it's excruciatingly important for us to get to know Sandy and Dawn O'Day."

"But how?" said Skinny-bones. "We've tried everything. We've stood around out back, and we've stood around out front, and every time Miss O'Day goes to empty her trash or to get in her car, she just smiles and waves and keeps on going."

"Yeah," said Rosie. "And we asked Mr. Reed, the mailman, if he'd let us deliver the mail, only he said it wasn't allowed, but that if we trailed along behind him *and* if Sandy barked *and* if Miss O'Day just happened to come to the door, he'd introduce us as his special helpers. Except that Sandy didn't bark, and Miss O'Day didn't come to the door, and Mr. Reed had to stuff the mail through the slot in the door and go on his way."

"And once we dressed up like characters from her books and marched up and down the street, and we even tried to make Mimi look like a golden retriever—and all that happened that time was that George Travis rode by and snatched my jewel-thief cape and never gave it back. And it was really Aunt Flossie's purple tablecloth, and she was mad as a wet hen."

"We'll think of something," said Rosie, crawling out from under the hydrangea bushes and blinking in the sunlight. "We *have* to."

"D'you think of anything yet?" said Skinny-bones, when the girls were finishing up their tuna-fish sandwiches at lunch.

"No, but I'm working on it," said Rosie.

"Think of what?" said Franny. "Working on what?"

"Getting to know Sandy," said Rosie.

"I already do," said Franny. "And now when I lean over the fence, he licks my hand."

"So what," said Rosie. "Anybody can get her hand licked, but what we want is to *really* know him. So we can be a part of his life."

"Part of his *life*?" said Miss Scott, rattling the ice in her glass of iced coffee. "You're sitting here thinking up ways for the two of you to be a part of some dog's life?"

"Not *some* dog, Aunt Flossie, but Sandy," said Skinny-bones.

"Sakes alive, but I hear more about Sandy these days than I hear about the President of the United States," said Miss Scott.

"Can I be a part of his life, too?" said Franny. " 'Cause if I can, then I'll help you think."

"Think first, and we'll let you know," said Rosie.

"Well . . ." said Franny. "You could give him a box of dog biscuits, with a ribbon on the top."

"That's dumb," said Rosie. "Sandy's got about a million dog biscuits. I know, because every morning Miss O'Day comes out back and gives him one, and then he eats it next to the birdbath."

"We could hire a skywriter," said Skinny-bones, "and get him to write 'Sandy the Super Dog' in big white letters over the house, and Miss O'Day'll come outside and see it before the letters squish up and fade away, and she'll know we did it and—"

"Skywriters cost money, and probably between the two of us we only have about a dollar," said Rosie. "But we could give him the key to the city, the way the mayor does when someone important comes to town."

"We don't *have* the key to the city," said Skinny-bones.

Rosie and Skinny-bones sat still. They listened to water dripping in the sink and to the hum of the refrigerator and thought of what to do next.

"If it's all that important to you, why don't you have a fair," said Miss Scott.

"A fair?" said Rosie.

"Yes, a fair," said Miss Scott. "Most everybody likes a fair. And you could take that ricky-ticky table out of our basement and set it up at the end of the driveway to put your things on."

"What things?" asked Skinny-bones.

"You know—the things that we're going to sell," said Rosie, suddenly excited and wishing that she had thought of having a fair herself. "We'll get a bunch of stuff and put it out for sale and make a big sign that says FAIR and invite all the neighbors up and down the street, including Miss Dawn O'Day—*ta-dum*—and Sandy the Super Dog." Rosie closed her eyes for a minute. She saw balloons blowing in the breeze and heard the music of a big brass band.

"You can have my button necklace to sell, if you let me keep the money," said Franny.

"There's a bunch of plastic daisies up to home that I'm not so much in need of anymore," said Miss Scott.

"And my pink net sachet with the smell mostly gone," said Skinny-bones.

"And I'll give my third-best Barbie doll," said Rosie. "The one where I chopped the hair off when I was little and thought that it would grow back, but it never did." She got up and went to the kitchen drawer for paper and pencil, coming back to the table to make a list. "And we'll call Mom at the Tree House and Dad at the office to see if they have anything. And Mimi'll donate her blue rubber ball—the one she hardly ever plays with—and Miss O'Day will come and buy it for Sandy, and then she'll invite us to come over and play ball with him."

"And we'll be a part of his life," said Skinny-bones.

"Yeah," said Rosie. She added up the things on her list, wrinkled her brow, and added them up again. "There's not enough," she said. "Not for a really splendiferous fair."

"We'll have to get more," said Skinny-bones. "We'll have to go to everybody's house and ask if they have anything for a worthy cause, and then we'll tell them about the fair and what time to come."

"Four o'clock," said Rosie.

"Can I go with you?" said Franny. "To get the things for the worthy cause?"

"I think I need you with me," said Miss Scott, getting up to put the dishes in the sink. "Let the girls go do their running around, and we'll just mosey up to my place and get that table from out of the cellar."

"The ricky-ticky table?" said Franny.

"The very one," said Miss Scott.

When Rosie and Skinny-bones went to Mrs. Corelli's house across the street, she gave them a jar of strawberry jam and told them she'd be happy to come to the fair. Miss Cook, in the house next door to the Riggses', found a paperback book with the cover torn off, and Mr. Buckley, at the corner, donated a paperweight in the shape of a duck. After Rosie called her parents at work, she went down to the cellar to get the green metal tray her mother told her she could have, and upstairs for her father's extra shoehorn from his dresser drawer. They set up the table at the end of the driveway and hung a sign that said FAIR across the front. They spread everything out: the jam, the book, and the paperweight; the Barbie doll with the cut-off hair, the net sachet, the plastic flowers; the tray, the shoehorn, and Franny's button necklace. And in the middle they put Mimi's blue rubber ball.

"There," said Rosie, standing back, with her hands on her hips.

"Yeah," said Skinny-bones, tugging at the sign to make it even.

"And now it's time to go and tell Miss O'Day about the fair."

The girls stood on the porch of the house next door twisting their feet and giggling and poking each other in the ribs. "You talk," said Rosie. "When she comes to the door, you talk."

"No, you," said Skinny-bones.

"It was your aunt who thought up the idea of the fair."

"But you're the one who wanted it to be splendiferous."

"I'll start, then," said Rosie. "I'll say the part about the fair, and you ask if she has anything she

wants to give. Then I'll say something else and you say something . . ."

"And then we're done," said Skinny-bones, reaching out to ring the bell.

As the bell rang inside the house, the girls watched as Sandy dashed into the hall, scrunching the rug under his feet, skidding on the floorboards, and jumping up to put his front paws against the long glass window next to the door. He barked and slobbered and wagged his tail.

"There he is—the fearless watchdog—just like in *Sandy's Baby-sitting Days*," said Skinny-bones.

"Except that he doesn't look like he thinks *we're* kidnappers, or even nefarious," said Rosie.

"Yeah, he's smiling, sort of. At least, I think he is," said Skinny-bones.

Just then Miss O'Day opened the door, pushing Sandy out of the way and telling him to sit. For a minute, the sound of his tail swishing against the floor filled the air.

"Go on," hissed Skinny-bones.

"In a minute," whispered Rosie. She cleared her throat, took a deep breath, and said, all in a rush, "My name is Rosie Riggs and this is Skinny-bones Scott who lives across the street and we're having a fair."

"And we wondered if you had anything you wanted to donate," said Skinny-bones.

Miss O'Day stood for a minute, scratching Sandy on the head and looking as if she were thinking of something far away. "Sorry, girls," she said after a while. "But I haven't really finished unpacking yet, and I don't know where anything is."

"But you'll come, won't you?" said Rosie.

"At four o'clock," said Skinny-bones.

" 'Cause there might be something you want to buy. For you, maybe, but definitely for Sandy."

"We'll see," said Miss O'Day as she shut the door.

At exactly four o'clock, Miss Cook came down the street with her white summer pocketbook over her arm. She stopped at the fair, picking up one thing and then another, ooohing and ahing. Finally she chose the jar of strawberry jam, paid for it, and started for home, her high heels clicking against the sidewalk.

George Travis spun around the corner, pulling his bike up into a wheelie, and calling, "Hey, Carrot Top—hey, Bean Pole—what'd'you got for me?"

"Nothing—and get away from here, George. We're having a fair," said Rosie.

"Ignore him," whispered Skinny-bones, taking a dime from Franny and handing her the bunch of plastic flowers.

Mrs. Corelli came next, buying the paperweight in the shape of a duck and saying it was what she had always wanted. Mr. Buckley chose the book *and* the shoehorn *and* the green metal tray.

"And I'll take that button necklace, if you please,"

said Miss Scott, dropping a quarter into the box.

"I want the net sachet," said Rosie, picking it up and breathing deeply, smelling the faraway scent of roses.

"And *I'll* buy the Barbie," said Skinny-bones.

Rosie and Skinny-bones looked down at the table, empty now except for Mimi's blue rubber ball.

Just then George Travis screeched into the driveway, coming so close that the girls saw the table shake and felt the breeze from his bike against their legs.

"What'd'you got left?" he said. "What's for me?"

"Nothing," said Rosie. "There's nothing left."

"How much is that ball?" said George.

"A dime," said Rosie, "but it's not for you. It's for somebody else."

"There isn't anybody else," said George.

Rosie and Skinny-bones looked up and down the deserted street. They looked over their shoulders at Sandy's house, at the door shut tight, and the empty porch.

"You can't *not* sell it to me," said George. "It's the law."

He flipped a coin up into the air and grabbed the ball and swung his bike around. Just then the back wheel caught the edge of the table, knocking it down and spilling the money so that coins rolled this way and that, across the driveway and into the grass.

-6-

Making Plans

"Do you think Dawn O'Day's feckless?" asked Rosie as she and her father scraped the plates and loaded the supper dishes into the dishwasher.

"No, why?" said Mr. Riggs.

"On account of she didn't come to the fair," said Rosie.

"Did she *say* she would? Did she *promise* and then not show up?"

"Noooooo," said Rosie, drawing the word out and not wanting to let it go.

"Well then," said Mr. Riggs, wiping at splatters of spaghetti sauce on the top of the stove. "I think feckless is when you promise something and don't do it, not when you don't do something you never said you'd do in the first place. If you get what I mean. It was a good fair, though, wasn't it?"

"Good," said Rosie, "but not splendiferous."

"Not too many things are. Splendiferous, I mean.

73

And if they were, then they wouldn't be splendiferous at all but just garden-variety good."

"Oh," said Rosie, thinking about what her father had said and figuring it out in her head. "Like they wouldn't be special?"

"Like they wouldn't be special," said Mr. Riggs.

"But we *wanted* it to be special," said Rosie. "Same as we wanted Dawn O'Day to come. Same as every day we want her to ask us over to play with Sandy, or to take him for a walk."

"Maybe Miss O'Day was busy," said her father.

"She didn't *look* busy," said Rosie. "She didn't act the way some people do when they answer the door and you can tell they'd rather be doing what they were doing before the bell rang."

"Maybe she was writing and was in the middle of a very exciting part and was afraid that if she stopped, she'd forget what was supposed to come next."

"She didn't *look* like she was in the middle of anything exciting," said Rosie. "I mean she looked like she always does, with her hair piled up on her head and a knitting needle going through the top —of her hair, not her head—and her face sort of calm and wrinkled."

"Or," Mr. Riggs went on, "maybe Miss O'Day is just plain shy."

"*Shy,*" said Rosie. "Grownups aren't shy."

"Sure they are," said Mr. Riggs. "The way some children are shy."

"I'm not," said Rosie, thinking how she waved her hand to answer in school, and always wanted a part in any play her class put on. "But Skinny-bones is," she said after a while. "Skinny-bones never wants to do anything out loud, and when we acted in *The Pied Piper of Hamelin* last year, all she wanted to be was a rat, 'cause there were lots of them, and she only wanted to be that because Mrs. Graham said everybody had to be something."

"There—you see," said her father. "Maybe when Dawn O'Day was little, she was like Skinny-bones."

Rosie closed her eyes and tried to think of Dawn O'Day as a little girl. Then she tried to think of Skinny-bones Scott as a grownup lady. "If I was a grownup, I wouldn't be shy," she said, sprinkling Comet in the sink and rubbing at it with the dishrag. "If I was a grownup, I'd *want* to be famous and I'd go *everywhere*—and to a million fairs up and down the street—and I'd let people take my picture and talk to me and write about me in newspapers."

"Yes, but that's you," said Mr. Riggs. "Lots of people aren't comfortable being in the limelight. Lots of people hate the idea of crowds and going places and being written up in big city papers."

"How about little ones?" said Rosie.

"Little ones what?" said her father.

"Little newspapers. Little tiny ones."

"Well, I don't know," said Mr. Riggs. "That might not be so bad."

"There, I've got it," said Rosie, swooshing water

in the sink, hanging up the rag, and wiping her hands down the sides of her shorts. "Hey and, Dad, thanks for the splendiferous idea."

Rosie ran through the living room, where her mother was reading "Cinderella" to Franny, calling back over her shoulder that she was going to Skinny-bones's, that she would be back before dark. She ran up the street, across Miss Scott's fake grass, past the plastic flowers, and up onto the porch. She pressed her face against the screen door and peered inside at Miss Scott and Skinny-bones, who were sitting on the couch watching *Wheel of Fortune*.

"Hey, Skinny-bones," Rosie called. "Guess what. I think Dawn O'Day wouldn't mind being written about in a little newspaper. That maybe she would say it was okay."

"What little newspaper?" said Skinny-bones.

"The one we're going to write," said Rosie.

The next morning, Rosie and Skinny-bones sat on the front porch planning their newspaper.

"We'll put the story about Sandy and Miss O'Day on the front page," said Rosie. "After we interview them, I mean. 'Cause that's the point—that we have to go and interview them, and Miss O'Day will ask us in and answer questions and tell us all kinds of things about her and Sandy that she's never told anybody before."

"Yeah," said Skinny-bones. "And then in the

back, on the second page, we'll put about Mrs. Corelli's trip to Italy and the Morgans moving away and how Miss Cook's sister came to visit. Stuff like that."

"Can I help?" said Franny, who sat on the bottom step pushing her wagon back and forth.

"No," said Rosie. "Except maybe later, when Mom gets home from the Tree House and takes us to get it Xeroxed, you can come."

Just then Skinny-bones poked her in the ribs and pointed to the wagon and rolled her eyes.

"*And*," said Rosie, "after *that* you can take your wagon and be our deliverer and go up and down the street and give everybody a paper."

"Is that important?" said Franny.

"Excruciatingly," said Rosie.

"Oh," said Franny. She got up and pulled her wagon down to the curb just as George Travis came by, calling, "Hey, Uglies, what're you doing now? Planning another fair?"

"They're planning a newspaper," said Franny. "And it's going to be all about that dog next door named Sandy the Super Dog, who's really *famous*, and I'm gonna get to deliver."

"That old dog?" said George, stopping his bike and putting one foot down on the ground. "Who'd want to write about him?"

"He's not an old dog," yelled Rosie. "He's Sandy the Super Dog, and he can do anything."

"Says who?" said George.

77

"Says me," said Skinny-bones, suddenly forgetting about never talking to George Travis. "He's in books and he has adventures and he goes places and everything."

"Hah," said George. "My yard backs up to his yard, and I see him all the time, and I know he's just a boring dog with worn places on his elbows. He just sleeps and walks around in circles, and now he has this plastic wading pool—whoever heard of a dog with a wading pool?"

"Maybe he's hot," said Rosie.

"Whatever you say, Hothead," said George. "And anyway, I bet a Martian could land right there, and he'd never even notice. Or a whole bunch of burglars could go into that house, and he wouldn't even bark."

"He would too," said Rosie. "If it was a Martian, he'd *eat* it, and if there were burglars, he'd chase them away."

"And if they took anything, he'd go after them and bring it back," said Skinny-bones.

"Fat chance, Fathead," said George, getting back on his bike and heading up the street, starting into a figure eight.

Rosie and Skinny-bones waited until Franny had gone around back and George was almost at the corner before they went next door to ask Dawn O'Day if they could interview her for their newspaper. They rang the bell and heard Sandy bark and watched as he scrunched the rug and slobbered on the window. When Miss O'Day opened the door, Rosie told her about the paper: that it was going to be only two pages long and not like a big city paper at all. Then Skinny-bones said they would like to ask her a few questions.

"Oh, girls, I *am* sorry," said Dawn O'Day. "And it's lovely of you to think of me. But I'm never very good with interviews, and I always say something incredibly silly, and then I wish I hadn't, so I've had to make it a practice never to talk to reporters, or to be in newspapers."

"Even us?" squeaked Skinny-bones.

"Even ours?" said Rosie.

"Even you—even yours," said Dawn O'Day, smiling so that the wrinkles creased across her face. "But thank you for asking."

After Dawn O'Day had closed the door, the girls stood on the porch for a minute without saying anything. Then Rosie sighed and said, "She was so nice about it, it was almost like she was saying yes the whole time she was saying no."

"Yeah," said Skinny-bones as they went down the steps and along the sidewalk.

"What happened?" said George, suddenly swooping up close to them. "Didn't Wonder Dog have anything to say?"

"It's not 'Wonder Dog,' " said Rosie. "It's 'Super Dog.' Sandy the Super Dog, stupid."

"Are you still having a newspaper? Do I still get to deliver?" said Franny, coming around the side of the house, her wagon bumping across the ground.

"No," said Rosie. "And go away."

When Skinny-bones and Miss Scott arrived at the Riggses' house the next morning, Rosie was waiting for them on the front porch. "Come on," she said, pulling Skinny-bones around to the back of the house. "Look," she said, pointing to a yellow scrubbing bucket overflowing with a can of Comet, a bottle of Windex, a roll of paper towels, and a jumble of sponges.

"What's that?" said Skinny-bones.

"A yellow scrubbing bucket."

"I know what it *is* but not what it's *for*," said Skinny-bones.

"It's my best, most exciting idea," said Rosie. "We'll ask Miss O'Day if she has any work she wants done, and when she says, 'What kind?' we'll say, 'Any kind.' We'll say we do windows and dust and scrub and weed the garden. Maybe even cut the grass, except that my father says I'm too little for the power mower."

"Windows?" said Skinny-bones. "Scrubbing? Dusting? Weeding?" She looked from Rosie down to the yellow bucket. "I don't much like doing windows 'cause, when I do them, Aunt Flossie comes along behind to see if there're any streaks. I don't much like scrubbing or dusting or weeding, either."

"We *have* to," said Rosie. "It's for a good cause. For Sandy."

"I guess," said Skinny-bones. "But just because it's Sandy, and only till we know him really well, and then we can quit and just be friends."

Rosie and Skinny-bones waited until Franny and Miss Scott were busy at the kitchen table playing lotto. They waited until George Travis was nowhere in sight and until they saw Miss O'Day come out into the back yard to fill the wading pool. Then they moved over close to the fence, holding the bucket between them.

"Hi, Miss O'Day," called Rosie. "It's us—Rosie Riggs and Skinny-bones Scott—and we thought maybe, on account of you just moved in, you might have work you wanted done."

"And we could do it," said Skinny-bones.

"We do anything."

"Almost anything."

"We do dusting and scrubbing and weeding."

"And sometimes windows," said Skinny-bones, making a face.

"We do excruciatingly good work, and we're never nefarious," said Rosie.

Dawn O'Day turned off the hose and dropped it on the ground. "Oh, girls, I'm sure you are excruciatingly good—and never nefarious," she said. "But I think I have everything under control as far as the house goes, and just this morning I hired someone to help me with the yard work. But thanks for offering." Then she picked up a beach ball, tossed it into the pool, and turned and went inside.

"It's not fair," said Rosie as she sat down on the back steps next to Skinny-bones.

"We should've got there sooner," said Skinny-bones.

"We should've gone to the front door and rung the bell like real business people," said Rosie.

"Now we're never going to get to know Sandy."

"Or be a part of his life."

"And we'll never be in a Sandy book or anything." Rosie poked at the yellow bucket with the toe of her tennis shoe and watched as it toppled over and rolled down the walk. She ran her fingers through her hair and thought that even with Skinny-bones here to play with instead of Ann, even with Sandy moving next door, this was still an abominable summer. She watched through the fence as Sandy got up from under the forsythia bush and wandered over to his wading pool, stepping in carefully, and then flopping, in a heap, into the water.

"Maybe George was right," she said.

"Right about what?" said Skinny-bones.

"About whoever heard of a dog having a wading pool. Why isn't he swimming in a river, or an ocean, or going over a waterfall in a barrel?" Rosie looked over at Sandy as he lay with his chin resting on the edge of the pool, his tail going *splash-plunk, splash-plunk* as it beat against the water.

Just then Miss Scott, followed by Franny with Mimi on a leash, came around the side of the house. "Come along now, girls," she said. "I need to pick up a few things at the store, and we're all going to walk along together so we can get back in time for lunch."

"Do we *have* to?" said Rosie. She wrapped her arms around her legs, pulling them back hard against the step and thinking how she wasn't walking down the street with any baby-sitter. At least, not with Miss Flossie Scott. Or Franny. Or Mimi. Or Skinny-bones either. "I'll just stay here," she said.

"Now, Rosie," said Miss Scott, "your mother doesn't pay for me to come here and leave you on your own."

"It'll be okay, I know it will. Mom does it all the time," said Rosie, crossing her fingers as she spoke.

"Does not," said Franny. "She hardly ever does."

"Okay or not, when I'm in charge, I want you to come with me," said Miss Scott.

Skinny-bones got up slowly and went to stand beside Franny. For a minute, Rosie looked at the three of them: at Franny in her father's T-shirt that hung down below her knees; at Skinny-bones in her brown school shoes without any socks; and at Miss Scott with her umbrella open, to keep the sun away, and her smiley-face tote bag hanging on her arm. She looked at Mimi, who was scratching a flea.

"If I have to go, I'm going incognito, then," said Rosie, wondering what she could do to make herself look less like Rosie Riggs and more like somebody else.

"There isn't time for incognito," said Miss Scott. "I want to get to the store to pick up some limes. I promised your mother I'd make her a Key lime pie one of these days—and this is as good a day as any, I venture." She hitched the tote bag higher on her arm, took Franny by the hand, and started down the driveway in a way that said she expected Rosie and Skinny-bones to follow along behind.

When they got almost to the end of the block, George Travis came around the corner, pushing a lawn mower and carrying a rake. "Hi, Uglies," he said. "How's the newspaper business?"

Suddenly Rosie felt cold all over. She caught hold of Skinny-bones, and together they watched as George trundled the mower down the street. They saw him stop in front of Dawn O'Day's house,

turn back toward them, and shake the rake over his head. "Oh, and, Uglies," he called, "I'll tell Wonder Dog you said hello."

"Now it's *really* not fair," said Rosie. She kicked at a tuft of grass and at a crack in the sidewalk. "George Travis at Dawn O'Day's house when it should've been *us*." She dragged her feet so that they burned through her tennis shoes. She picked up a stone and threw it hard at a tree.

Suddenly Franny was there, dancing around her and tangling her in Mimi's leash. "Rosie's mad, and I am glad," she sang. "Rosie's a pain and a crab and a pickle puss rolled into one."

"I am not," said Rosie, drawing herself up as tall as she could. "I'm cantankerous, is all."

"What's 'can-tan-ker-ous'?" said Franny.

"Cross, and sort of cranky," said Skinny-bones.

"That's what I said," said Franny. "A pain and a crab and a pickle puss rolled into one."

— 7 —

The Storm

The sky was dark and heavy and streaked with yellow when Rosie, Franny, and their father went outside after supper.

"It looks like a bruise," said Rosie. "The way a bruise gets after it's stopped being black and blue."

"Yes," said her father. "And we won't have to water the lawn tonight."

"Is it going to rain?" said Franny.

"Looks that way," said Mr. Riggs. He walked down the yard, checking his rose bushes and pulling at an occasional weed. Mimi went along with him for a while, then turned and came back, settling onto the sidewalk for a nap.

"It's weird out here and sort of like the world's holding its breath," said Rosie. She sat on the steps, watching the wind chimes in the Bradford pear tree hanging straight and still.

"The calm before the storm," said Mr. Riggs.

"But not for Sandy. See what he's doing." Rosie looked through the fence as Sandy paced back and forth. She heard him whimper, then saw him paw at the ground, and finally burrow deep under his favorite forsythia bush.

"Maybe he's afraid of the storm coming up. Dogs can sense these things," said her father.

"No," said Rosie. "Sandy's not afraid. Sandy *loves* storms. He's not a wimp, or a coward either. And he doesn't mind a little adversity."

"I'm sure he doesn't—but he could still be afraid of storms."

"Like you're afraid of worms," said Franny. "And you're not a wimp or a coward or mind a little— what you said."

"Adversity—it's a kind of trouble," said Rosie. "Anyway, I'm *not* afraid of worms. I just think they're gross, is all."

There was a distant rumble of thunder, and Sandy pushed his way out from under the bush and raced across the yard. He barked and whined and clawed at the back door until Miss O'Day let him in.

"See—he *is* scared," said Franny. "Sandy's scared and I'm not, and that makes me braver than Sandy the Super Dog." She hopped up the steps on one foot and stood balancing herself just above her sister.

"Liar," said Rosie. "The only reason you're acting

so brave is 'cause Dad's here *with* you. And so am I. And Mom's right inside."

"You're just can-tan-ker-ous," said Franny.

"Am not."

"Are too. You said you were this afternoon when we saw George Travis going in Sandy's house, where you wanted to be."

"I was then, but I'm not anymore. That shows what you know."

"Pain."

"Baby."

"Crab."

"Pig snot."

"Pickle puss."

Rosie turned to grab Franny's leg just as the younger girl swung back in a kick, and suddenly the two of them rolled off the steps, across the walk, and into the grass, pushing and pulling at each other as they went.

"That's *enough*," said Mr. Riggs as the sound of thunder filled the air, making his voice seem louder than it ever had before. "Now both of you go to your rooms, until you cool off a bit."

Upstairs, Rosie's room was thick with shadows and darker than it usually was at this time of day. She turned on the light, and then the radio, listening to the crackle of static that filled the air. She sat on the bed, picking up her thesaurus and flipping through it, trying to find a word that described how she felt. " 'Cantankerous' is the best there is," she said under her breath. She looked in the back of the book, then turned to number 951 and read, "*Cross—cranky—mean—ornery—huffy.* But it doesn't say anything about being a pain or a crab or a pickle puss, either one."

There was a sudden clap of thunder, and Rosie pushed the book under her pillow and got up, moving over to the window and watching as the trees and bushes twisted in the wind. She heard a door slam downstairs and, from the back yard, the jangling of the wind chimes. Lightning streaked the sky, and Rosie jumped back, looking over her shoulder. She moved over to the door, looking at the light spilling out into the hall, seeing her sister standing just inside her own room.

"Hi," said Rosie.

"Hi," said Franny.

"You scared?" said Rosie.

"No—yes," said Franny.

"Me too—a little," said Rosie. "Dad said to go to our rooms, but he didn't say we couldn't talk."

"Or play beanbag," said Franny. She tossed her beanbag in the shape of a frog across the hall to Rosie, who tossed it back again. Then both girls sat down, each in her own doorway, each with her legs spread far apart, and slid the beanbag back and forth between them. *Zip* went the beanbag, *zip—*

zip—zip, as Rosie and Franny leaned forward, concentrating on what they were doing and trying not to hear the storm raging outside.

The thunder rolled and roared overhead. There was a sharp crack as the lights blinked and then went out.

And suddenly Rosie and Franny were in the middle of the hall, yelling and hanging on to each other, feeling their way along the wall and down the stairs.

"Mommy—Daddy," called Franny.

"The lights went out, and it's dark up there," said Rosie.

"It's dark down here, too," said Franny, her teeth chattering as she spoke.

"And outside," said Rosie, looking through the open front door to the darkness beyond.

"It's all right, girls," said Mrs. Riggs, coming in from the kitchen and carrying two candles that turned the room an orangy-yellow. "The storm knocked the power out, but we have plenty of candles."

Rosie watched the shadows dancing and lunging on the walls and across the ceiling. She saw the shapes of furniture and the outlines of the windows and heard the thunder rumbling overhead. Just then her father came up from the cellar carrying a flashlight, playing it around the room and deep into the corners. "This's just to show you that

everything's all right," he said. "But I'll turn it off now to save the batteries."

Rosie sat on the couch next to Mimi and stared at the flickering candle flames. "It's weird," she said. And scary too, she thought.

"What'll we *do*?" said Franny.

"We could tell ghost stories," said Rosie, not at all sure that this was a good idea.

"No—no ghost stories," said Franny. "Something funny."

"I have a joke, then," said Mr. Riggs, clearing his throat and saying, "Where was Moses when the lights went out?"

"Upstairs?" said Franny.

"In the bathroom?" said Rosie.

"Think, girls," said their mother in a voice that said she'd heard this joke about a hundred times.

"Where?" said Rosie and Franny.

"In the dark," said their father.

"Oh," said Rosie.

"I don't get it," said Franny.

"That's it—that's all there is. Where was Moses when the lights went out—in the dark," said Rosie. "Now do you get it?"

"I guess," said Franny. "But mine're better." Then Franny told seven knock-knock jokes all in a row.

After the rain stopped and the storm moved on, Rosie, Franny, and their parents went outside. Mrs. Riggs wiped the porch furniture with a towel and lit the green and yellow bug candles on the table. Rosie sat on the top step, feeling the damp wood through her shorts and listening to the water gurgling in the downspouts. She looked up at the sky and down at the darker shapes of trees and houses and lampposts lining the street. She heard Mr. Buckley call across to the Corellis that he had telephoned the gas and electric company, that they would have the power on as soon as possible. She saw the flicker of candles from front steps and porches and, suddenly, a single headlight as George Travis zigzagged his bike down the street and disappeared around the corner.

"Hey, Rosie," yelled Skinny-bones from the end of her walk. "Hey, Rosie," she yelled again, swinging her light back and forth so that the dark was splotched with yellow. "Come on over."

Rosie grabbed her father's flashlight and ran down to the sidewalk, blinking it on and off and calling, "No—you come up here. I'll meet you partway." She waited until she saw Skinny-bones and Miss Scott coming closer, carrying a lantern between them, then made her way along the sidewalk, holding the flashlight close and stepping into its beam. When she got in front of Sandy's house, she saw a dark shadow sitting on the front steps. "Hi," said Rosie, waving her flashlight. "It's me—Rosie."

"Hi, Rosie," answered the shadow in Dawn O'Day's voice.

*　*　*

Miss Scott settled onto the porch swing next to Mrs. Riggs, and for a few minutes the grownups talked about the storm and the power being off and how long it would be before the food spoiled in the refrigerators and freezers up and down the street.

. "And to think that I bought ice cream today," said Mrs. Riggs.

"It's a bother," said Miss Scott.

"It's horrendous," said Rosie.

"What's 'hor-ren-dous'?" said Franny.

"The storm and the lights being out, but mostly the ice cream mushing in the freezer," said Rosie.

"No—what's it *mean*?" said Franny.

"Awful," said Skinny-bones.

"And horrible, both at the same time," said Rosie.

"Now, wait a minute, girls," said Mr. Riggs. "I think that maybe in the broad scheme of things Miss Scott's right—this is a bother, but hardly horrendous."

"It is to me," said Rosie, thinking of a large puddle of ice cream spreading slowly over the bottom of the freezer. "And I bet it is to Dawn O'Day, too, sitting over there on her steps all in the dark without even any candles. I bet that's horrendous."

"Dawn O'Day?" said Mrs. Riggs.

"In the dark?" said Mr. Riggs.

And all of a sudden Rosie remembered her father's joke. Where was Miss O'Day when the lights went out? she asked herself. In the dark, she answered herself.

"But that's terrible," said Mrs. Riggs.

"I told you it was horrendous," said Rosie. "Except, of course, that she has Sandy." She tried not to think of the way Sandy had whined and scratched at the door when he heard the thunder.

"Yes—but we should still ask her to come over," said her mother. "And we could lend her some candles."

"I'll go and get her," said Mr. Riggs, picking up the flashlight. "Anybody want to come with me?"

"We do," said Rosie, jumping off the porch rail. "Me and Skinny-bones. And Franny," she said, catching her father's look in the flickering candle-light.

Mr. Riggs went up the walk of the house next door, herding Rosie and Skinny-bones and Franny in front of him, shining the light on the sidewalk and calling, "Is that you, Miss O'Day? Is that you there in the dark?"

"Indeed it is—and glad to see some familiar faces—and feeling like a fool. Can you believe I don't have a single candle in the house, and my flashlight seems to have been lost in the move."

"Well, come over with us, then. We're all sitting

out on the porch—Joan, and Miss Scott from down the street, and my three friends here. We have plenty of candles, and we'll give you some to bring home."

"Thanks, I will," said Miss O'Day, getting up off the steps. "Just let me get my key and lock the door."

"Can Sandy come?" said Rosie, the words popping out before she knew she was going to say them.

"Sandy? Well, if I can find him, he can. I hate to say it, but Sandy's a dreadful scaredy-pie where storms are concerned, and right now he's probably under the bed, or maybe even in the bathtub," said Miss O'Day, her voice sounding as if *under the bed* and *in the bathtub* were the best possible places to be. She opened the screen door and went in calling, "San-dy, you, San-dy," and when she came out, the dog was with her, pressing close to her side while Miss O'Day locked the door and followed Mr. Riggs and the girls down the walk.

When they got back to the Riggses' house, Mimi came running down off the porch, yapping at Sandy, jumping at him. Sandy poked at her with his nose, and together the two dogs sniffed each other, moving in circles on the grass.

"That's all right, they're just getting to know each other," said Dawn O'Day as she went to sit on the porch.

"I'm glad I'm not a dog," said Rosie. "I'm glad I don't have to get to know people by *smelling* them."

"Yeah," said Skinny-bones. "People like strangers and school principals and George Travis."

"That's gross," said Rosie.

"And hor-ren-dous?" said Franny.

"And horrendous," said Skinny-bones.

Franny went to sit with her mother and Miss Scott on the swing, and Mimi curled up on the doormat and went to sleep. For a few minutes, Sandy wandered around the porch, nudging at shadows and into corners, then finally coming over and flopping down on the top step, wedging his head and front paws between Rosie and Skinny-bones.

Rosie caught her breath. Me and Sandy, she thought. Me and Sandy the Super Dog. She felt the warmth of the big dog next to her, and she put her hand down on his head, scratching him behind the ears. She heard the grownups behind her calling one another Tom and Joan and Dawn and Flossie. She heard them talking about books and movies; about what was going on in the world. She listened to the night noises and thought how they sounded louder in the dark.

Just then Sandy put his head up, cocking his ears and looking straight ahead.

"Do you think he hears something?" said Skinny-bones.

"Maybe," said Rosie. "Or else he's thinking."

"About something exciting."

"And daring."

"And incredibly brave."

"About what to do next," said Rosie.

– 8 –

Where's Sandy?

Rosie woke to the sound of her radio playing "Stars and Stripes Forever" and to the sight of the lamp on her bedside table shining brightly. "What's that?" she said to her mother, who had come in to turn them off.

"Just the electricity going back on," said Mrs. Riggs. "And now everything that went *off* when the power went off is *on* again. But go back to sleep. It's early yet."

"How early?"

"Five o'clock," said Mrs. Riggs.

"Five o'clock in the *morning*?" said Rosie, sitting up and looking at the thin, watery light coming in the window. But her mother was already on her way downstairs, where Rosie could hear the stereo blaring.

"Five o'clock in the morning is an excruciatingly horrendous time of day—except for birds," muttered Rosie, lying down and pulling the sheet up, liking the way it felt cool and damp against her shoulders. For a few minutes, she listened to the birds twittering outside. She scrunched her pillow under her head and settled in to go back to sleep. Then suddenly she remembered the night before, and her eyes opened wide. "It *did* happen," she said out loud. "Me and Skinny-bones and Sandy the Super Dog sitting on my front porch." She remembered how her mother had served the ice cream to keep it from melting in the freezer, and how afterward they had all walked Dawn O'Day and Sandy home and waited out front while Miss O'Day lit the candles and went inside. And she remembered how, just as Miss O'Day was about to close the door, she had called out, "Oh, Rosie and Skinny-bones, why don't you come over tomorrow and play with Sandy. I'm sure he'd love the company."

"And we will," said Rosie, feeling herself drifting off to sleep. "Later, when Skinny-bones gets here and it's really day and not five o'clock in the morning."

When Rosie woke the next time, the sun was shining and the room was hot and stuffy. She pushed the pillow away, stretched her arms up over her head, and took up the Sandy thoughts where she had left off. First Skinny-bones'll come here, Rosie told herself, and then we'll go next door to see Sandy, and for a while we'll play with him in the yard, with his ball and his wading pool, and maybe even under the forsythia bush. Then, after he gets used to us some more, we'll take him for a walk, and Sandy'll wear his red bandanna, and kids along the street and over by the swimming pool will see us and follow us and yell out, "Hey— isn't that Sandy the Super Dog? Can we have his paw print?" And Skinny-bones and I will turn and smile and sort of bow and say, "Sandy has to have his exercise now—to keep in shape for his next great adventure."

And some day in September, Rosie's thoughts went on, Miss O'Day will let us take Sandy to school and kids'll be lined up and down the halls and in the library and the multipurpose room, waving and going "Ahhhhh." Then last year's teacher and this year's teacher and the principal and the librarian and the nurse who is sometimes cantankerous will say, "Isn't it splendiferous to have a dog in school."

Just at that moment the doorbell rang, and Rosie heard her mother hurry to answer it. "That's Aunt Kate's voice," Rosie said to herself, jumping out of bed and going to lean over the railing in the hall, listening as her mother and aunt went into the kitchen. She tiptoed over to the door of Franny's room, peering inside to make sure that her sister was still asleep, then crept carefully down the steps, jumping the last three and racing through the dining room and into the kitchen. "Ta-dum," she said, stopping in front of Aunt Kate and taking a deep breath before she went on. "Here you have before you someone who sat on her own front porch last night with—Sandy the Super Dog. That's on account of the lights went out, and Dawn O'Day was all in the dark like Moses, and Dad and Skinny-bones and I went over to get her and Sandy. And once they got here, Dawn O'Day talked like everybody else, so maybe what Dad said before about her being shy was true. Only she isn't anymore."

"Fantastic," said Aunt Kate. "How was the visit?"

"Fantastic," said Rosie. She sat down next to Aunt Kate and told her how Dawn O'Day had said for her and Skinny-bones to come over and play with Sandy. She was just at the part about maybe someday taking Sandy to school when the phone rang.

"Hello," said Mrs. Riggs, handing Aunt Kate a cup of coffee as she answered it.

"Oh no," she went on in what Rosie knew was her mother's something-wrong voice. "Oh, that's dreadful. When did you find this out? I'll be right over, and we can try to decide what to do," said Mrs. Riggs, hanging up the phone.

"What's wrong, Joan?" said Aunt Kate.

"It's Sandy," said Mrs. Riggs. "He's missing."

"Missing?" said Aunt Kate.

"Yes. Dawn put him in the yard when she got up this morning, and when she looked out a few minutes later, he wasn't there. She's been all around the neighborhood and still hasn't found him. I told her I'd come over, if you don't mind staying here at least till Franny's up and the girls are dressed. Then we'll all have to help look."

Skinny-bones knocked on the back screen door just as Mrs. Riggs started out. "Oh, Skinny-bones, come on in," she said. "Rosie will tell you what's happened."

"What's happened?" said Skinny-bones.

"Sandy's missing," said Aunt Kate.

"Sandy's missing," said Rosie, wiggling her eyebrows.

"Missing?" said Skinny-bones, wiggling her eyebrows back again.

"Yes, missing," said Aunt Kate. She looked carefully from Rosie to Skinny-bones before she said, "I can't imagine how he could have gotten out of that fenced yard. Can you?"

"Hmm—mmm," said Rosie, shrugging her shoulders.

"Hmm—mmm," said Skinny-bones, shrugging *her* shoulders.

Rosie took a box of cereal out of the cupboard and hummed a tune as she poured two bowls and handed one to Skinny-bones.

"Girls, don't you hear what we've been saying?" said Aunt Kate. "Sandy's missing."

"We heard," said Rosie.

"We heard," said Skinny-bones.

"But you don't seem very upset," said Aunt Kate. "What do you know that the rest of us don't know?"

"Nothing," said Rosie.

"Except that he's Sandy, and he can do anything," said Skinny-bones.

"And last night, when we were out on the porch and Sandy was sitting there between us, he held up his head and looked straight out into the dark, and we just knew he was thinking of what he was going to do next. Like white-water rafting or going out West or maybe even to Alaska."

"And if he's not there this morning, that's only because he's gone to *do* it."

"On account of him being the Super Dog and all," said Rosie.

"But, girls, don't you understand that Sandy doesn't even know the neighborhood? That Miss O'Day must be frantic?" said Aunt Kate.

"Why?" said Rosie. "She knows he can do anything."

"And find his way to anywhere and back again," said Skinny-bones.

Aunt Kate went to the stove and filled her coffee cup. She came back to the table, sitting down and looking carefully from one girl to the other. And when she spoke, her words came slowly, with lots of spaces in between. "This is a lovable old *dog* we're talking about here. Somebody's pet. Surely you both understand that it's not just some super dog who lives in books and Dawn O'Day's imagination."

"Imagination?" said Rosie, her voice cracking as she said the word.

"Yes, Rosie. You know about imagination: about making more out of something than was there to begin with. We've talked about it ourselves, and so have some of the writers who've come to the Tree House."

"Ye-es," said Rosie, "but then when I go to put it into words, I can't exactly. Maybe you'd better explain it again. So Skinny-bones'll understand."

Aunt Kate sat back, looking up at the ceiling and pushing her hands through her hair. "Imagination," she said, "is like having wings on your thoughts.

"Imagination changes a crack on a wall into a rabbit, a shadow into an ogre, and a cloud into a dragon.

"It makes rain on a summer night sound like music, and thunder like angels moving furniture overhead.

"It turns a frog into a prince and an everyday kind of a dog into a super dog."

"You mean he isn't a super dog?"

"He is, of course he is," said Aunt Kate. "But you know why, don't you?"

Rosie thought for a while, not sure of what she

was thinking; not sure she *liked* what she was thinking. "You mean that all of Sandy's adventures are on account of Dawn O'Day and her imagination? But that can't be true. Dawn O'Day's just like anybody else. She's sort of wrinkly with fat knees and wears bare feet around the house and has knitting needles in her hair."

"That's the nice thing about an imagination," said Aunt Kate. "You don't have to be anything special to have one. You don't have to be young enough or old enough or rich or beautiful enough. You can be wrinkly and walk in your bare feet and have knitting needles in your hair. You can even have *gray* hair and fat knees. All you have to do is look and wait and listen and believe in all kinds of things. And that's pretty magical in itself, when you come to think of it."

Rosie sighed, and Skinny-bones sighed.

"I wish I had one," said Rosie.

"You do, Rosie-posie, you do," said Aunt Kate, laughing a laugh that sounded to Rosie as light as the wings on a butterfly.

"And now," said Aunt Kate, getting up to rinse the dishes and put them in the dishwasher, "let's make some plans here. I'll go wake Franny, and, Rosie, you get dressed, and, Skinny-bones, why don't you think of all the places we can look for Sandy."

While Rosie put on shorts and a shirt and tied her tennis shoes, Skinny-bones sat on her bed, looking at the Sandy poster. "Do you think what your aunt said is true?" she asked.

"Sort of, and sort of not," said Rosie. "I mean, writers do *think* of things, and make them up, and use their imaginations, but still . . ."

"There's Sandy," said Skinny-bones.

"A real live dog, and I just *know* last night when we were all sitting on the steps that Sandy was thinking of *something*," said Rosie. "Something exciting, and sort of splendiferous."

She went over and stopped by the window, looking down into the yard next door. She saw Sandy's empty wading pool and his favorite forsythia bush. She saw his water bowl, his beach ball, and his blue rubber ring toy. And all of a sudden Rosie felt a funny pain right in the middle of her stomach. "But Sandy *is* gone," she said.

"Yeah," said Skinny-bones.

"And maybe what Aunt Kate said about him not knowing the neighborhood is true," said Rosie.

"So maybe we'd better *look*," said Skinny-bones.

"Just in case," said Rosie.

When Rosie and Skinny-bones got back downstairs, Mrs. Riggs and Dawn O'Day were waiting with Franny and Aunt Kate.

"Sandy's missing," said Franny. "And he needs

his medicine, and sometimes he's afraid of traffic, and I get to go in the car with Mom and Miss O'Day to look for him."

"We'll drive up to the avenue and over to the shopping center," said Mrs. Riggs. "And, Rosie, why don't you and Skinny-bones take Mimi and walk all around the neighborhood. She can help you look. We'll all meet back here in half an hour."

"Take *Mimi?*" said Rosie. She started to tell her mother that that was an excruciatingly *bad* idea: that Mimi had short stubby legs and couldn't walk fast and wouldn't be able to look for *anyone*. But just then she looked at Dawn O'Day and saw the little lines of worry crinkling her face, saw the way she clasped and unclasped her hands.

"Okay," said Rosie, sighing and reaching for the leash. "We'll go, and we'll take Mimi."

"And I'll stay here, in case Sandy comes back on his own," said Aunt Kate.

– 9 –

How Mimi Helped

Out on the sidewalk, Mimi stopped to sniff a bush, a rock, and a fire hydrant. She dug at the ivy in front of Miss Cook's house, chased a butterfly, and wound the leash around Skinny-bones's legs.

"If Mimi were a bloodhound," said Rosie, untangling the leash, "we'd give her something of Sandy's to smell, and she'd take off over fences and under hedges and around corners, and we'd take off after her, and then finally she'd screech to a stop and there'd be Sandy, just waiting for us to find him."

"Yeah," said Skinny-bones. "I saw it once in a cartoon. But Mimi's not a bloodhound, so we'll have to look."

"And call."

"And ask people up and down the street."

Rosie and Skinny-bones looked in the Corellis' side yard and under the hydrangea bush in front of Mr. Buckley's porch. They pushed open the door of the Riggses' garage and called "Sandy—Sandy." They called "Biscuit" and, sometimes, "Baloney," just in case he might be hungry.

They saw Miss Cook working in her garden and stopped to ask if she had seen Sandy. "Sandy?" said Miss Cook. "I don't believe I know any Sandy."

"He's a golden retriever, and a Super Dog," said Skinny-bones.

"I don't believe I know any Super Dog either," said Miss Cook.

"But you must," said Rosie. "He lives in the Morgans' old house, except now he's missing."

"Oh, dear," said Miss Cook, pulling up a weed and dropping it into her basket. "If I see him, I'll tell him you were asking after him."

Next the girls went down to Skinny-bones's house to tell Miss Scott that Sandy had disappeared and to ask her to watch for him as she swept her sidewalk and squirted her plastic flowers with a hose. They talked to the mailman, to the garbage man, and to a woman walking a baby, asking if they had seen Sandy: telling them about his red bandanna and the way he held his head and how his tail went *splash-plunk* when he wagged it in the wading pool.

"You know what I think?" said Skinny-bones when the mailman, the garbage man, and the woman walking the baby had all shaken their heads and gone on. "I think we need a picture of Sandy to carry with us. That way we can just hold it up and show it to people like the guys from the FBI do on television when they're looking for a bank robber."

"Or a jewel thief going incognito," said Rosie.

"Yeah," said Skinny-bones, "and then we won't have to keep saying the same thing over all the time. Let's go home and get a book with Sandy on the cover and carry it with us."

"*Or*," said Rosie, holding her arms out wide, "let's take the poster. The one off my bedroom wall, and every time we see someone, we'll unroll it and hold it up and say, 'Have you seen this dog?' Anyway, Mom said to be back in half an hour, and it's probably half an hour already."

When Rosie and Skinny-bones got back to the Riggses' house, Sandy wasn't there.

"We drove to the shopping mall, and around the parking lot and over by the school," said Mrs. Riggs.

"We yelled '*Sandy*' out the window," said Franny.

"I know he's been kidnapped," said Dawn O'Day, pacing the floor. "Or dognapped. Or hit by a car."

"Have you tried the pound?" said Aunt Kate. "Maybe he got loose and was picked up by the dogcatcher. Or maybe someone found him and didn't know where he lived."

"We're going there next," said Mrs. Riggs. "I know you have to get over to the Tree House,

Kate, and I wanted to tell Rosie and Skinny-bones where we'd be—and to go down to Miss Scott's when they're finished looking."

"We'll *never* be finished until we find Sandy," said Rosie. Then, calling "Wait there" and "Don't leave yet" over her shoulder, she ran up the steps and down again, carrying the Sandy poster and stopping to bend back the little pieces of Scotch tape that stuck out all around it.

"See," said Rosie, going to stand in front of Dawn O'Day and holding the poster up in front of her. "We're taking this with us."

"And showing it to everyone we see," said Skinny-bones.

"And they'll all tell a bunch more other people."

"Till everybody for miles around is saying, 'Sandy—Sandy—Sandy—' "

"And Sandy'll hear, wherever he is," said Rosie.

"And then be found," said Skinny-bones.

For a minute, Miss O'Day blinked and swallowed hard. She rubbed at her eyes and gave Rosie and Skinny-bones a quick hug before she followed Mrs. Riggs outside to the car.

Rosie and Skinny-bones took Mimi and went along to where Miss Cook was still working in her garden. They unrolled the poster and held it up, just in case she didn't know what a Super Dog *or* a golden retriever looked like. They went around the corner, then around another corner, holding the poster out between them and calling, *"Have you seen this dog?"* They showed it to a woman painting a picket fence and to a boy delivering meat for Meyer's Meat Market.

They walked down one side of the street and back up the other side, past George Travis's house, where they heard a loud "Psssssst," coming from behind the hedge.

"Pssssssst," came the voice again. "Hey, Uglies—hey, you guys. Are you looking for Sandy?"

"Yeah," said Skinny-bones.

"How'd you know that?" said Rosie.

"I've got ears," said George. "I heard you going up and down the street yelling, 'Have you seen this dog?'—and there's *your* dog, Carrot Top, and Bean Pole doesn't have one."

"It could be some other dog," said Rosie.

"It could be *any* dog," said Skinny-bones.

"So how'd you know it was Sandy?" said Rosie.

"I didn't, exactly," said George.

Rosie held the poster over her head and pushed her way through the hedge. "Come on, Skinny-bones, bring Mimi and come in the gate. He *knows* something."

"I was just guessing," said George. "I thought maybe."

"You knew it all along, didn't you, George?"

"No."

"Yes."

"I could help you look, though," said George.

"Help *us* look?" said Skinny-bones. "When Sandy's gone and it's probably all your fault, George Travis."

"It was an accident," said George.

"What was?" said Rosie.

"Sandy being gone." George took a step back, and then another, and another. He turned, pointing to the fence at the end of his yard. "See that fence? It's between our yard and Sandy's, and sometimes when I'm throwing the basketball, he comes over and puts his paws on it and sort of watches. Only this morning I was eating a chocolate doughnut, and Sandy kept sniffing and leaning across, and I held it close to see what he'd do, and then all of a sudden he was sort of scrambling up the fence to the top, and then he was all the way on this side, and I gave him the doughnut, and that was okay."

"So where is he?" said Rosie.

"That's just it," said George, his voice squeaking on the "it."

"What is?" said Skinny-bones.

"Where is he?" said Rosie.

"He's gone," said George.

"Gone?" said Rosie, climbing on an overturned wheelbarrow and stabbing her rolled-up poster in George's direction. "What do you mean, *gone*?"

"That's what I'm trying to *tell* you," said George. "Well, first Sandy came over the fence, and then he ate the doughnut, and then he just sort of hung out. You know, sniffing and rolling in the grass and digging, like he does." He pointed to a hole in Mrs. Travis's rose bed before going on. "And, after he'd been here awhile, I started showing him stuff—my bike and my skateboard, my cap gun."

"Your cap gun?" said Skinny-bones.

"You didn't shoot it, did you?" said Rosie. "You didn't shoot that cap gun at Sandy?"

"Not *at* him, just sort of next to him, but up in the air," said George. "And all of a sudden he was gone. I mean, that dog went through the gate and down the street. We're talking *fast.*"

"And didn't you go after him?" said Rosie.

"I did," said George. "I rode my bike, but I couldn't find him, and then I came back here and waited by the fence, watching, 'cause I figured he'd go to *his* yard. Him being a wonder dog and all."

"Super Dog," said Skinny-bones. "He's Sandy the Super Dog."

"Except that he's afraid of noises—of thunder and explosions and cap guns. Same as I'm the tiniest bit afraid of worms," said Rosie.

"And me of vampire movies," said Skinny-bones.

Rosie handed the poster to Skinny-bones and climbed from the wheelbarrow to the top of the picnic table. She put her hands on her hips and took a deep breath, ready to tell George that he had been feckless. That shooting the cap gun anywhere near Sandy had been an abominable thing to do. She looked down at George, and all of a sudden he looked smaller than he ever had before. His face was white and splotched with red, his eyes open wide. There were poison-ivy blisters on his legs.

I'd like to keep him that way, thought Rosie. It'd be like pushing the stop button on the VCR and having George stuck there forever, and he'd never be able to throw eggs on houses or toilet-paper the trees. And he couldn't call me Carrot Top or Skinny-bones Bean Pole. And he wouldn't be able to shoot his cap gun and scare Sandy ever again. She closed her eyes and licked her lips.

Then Rosie remembered Sandy. She remembered that he was still missing; that maybe, in spite of being the Super Dog, he was scared and lonely and didn't know his way home. That they had to find him.

She opened her eyes and blinked. She saw Mimi jump up, pawing the air, and George Travis picking at his poison ivy. She heard Skinny-bones say, "Come on, Rosie, let's look for Sandy."

"Me too?" said George.

Rosie and Skinny-bones looked at each other. They looked at George.

"We—ll," said Rosie.

"You could help, maybe," said Skinny-bones.

"On account of you were the one who let Sandy get lost, sort of," said Rosie.

"And as long as you remember that we're in charge—that we're the main lookers. Dawn O'Day said so," said Skinny-bones.

"And you stop saying 'Wonder Dog' when you know right well he's a *Super* Dog," said Rosie.

"And you promise never to call *us* Carrot Top and Bean Pole ever again," said Skinny-bones.

"Yeah. Sure. Okay," said George. "Anything you say, Uglies," he whispered under his breath as he followed Rosie and Skinny-bones out of the yard and down the street.

Rosie and Skinny-bones and George went over to the next block, and then to the block after that. The only people they saw were the woman pushing a stroller and an old man pulling a bulldog in a red coaster wagon. They walked down to the swimming pool, talking to the girl at the gate, showing her the poster, and asking if she had seen Sandy. They sat on the curb, stretching their legs out into the street, and tried to decide what to do next.

"We could go to the post office and hang that poster on the wall next to the ones that say *Wanted*," said George.

"*No,*" said Rosie. "Those are nefarious criminals

on the wall of the post office, and Sandy's not. Sandy's—well, he's Sandy, and we can't put him there with the bad guys."

"If we had a whole bunch of posters, we could hang one on every lamppost, and then people'd see them, and somebody would find him and bring him home," said Skinny-bones.

"Except that we don't have a whole bunch of posters but just this one, and besides, there aren't any people on account of everybody's either at the pool or inside or at work."

"Or in their back yards," said George.

"Back yards?" said Rosie.

"Yeah," said George. "Like I was when Sandy came over the fence and ran away. Like my mother is when she works on her roses."

"And Aunt Flossie when she hangs out the clothes," said Skinny-bones.

"Back yards," said Rosie, getting up and pulling on Mimi's leash, "Come on, let's go."

George raced out in front, giving a war whoop as he rounded the corner. Rosie and Skinny-bones ran to catch up.

"Get back, George Travis. Get back," shouted Rosie.

"We said we were in charge. That we were the main lookers," said Skinny-bones.

"It was my idea," said George.

"It's on account of you that Sandy got away."

They went along the middle of the street, their feet making thunking noises as they ran. They went down driveways and in and out of back yards. They saw clothes flapping on the line. They saw swing sets and picnic tables and outdoor grills. They saw birdbaths and cellar doors.

They went out front again and stopped on the sidewalk next to a lamppost, gasping and holding their sides. Mimi rolled onto the grass with her tongue hanging out. All of a sudden she jumped up, standing with her feet far apart, her head tilted to the side. She tugged at the end of the leash, pulling Rosie down a driveway, past a Jeep and a jumble of bicycles, and through a gate that was hanging open.

They stopped just inside the yard, looking at the sliding board, the sandbox, the toys scattered on the grass. Mimi barked and yanked at the leash again, heading up to the corner of the yard, to the green plastic wading pool.

"Sandy!" shrieked Rosie.

"Sandy!" shrieked Skinny-bones and George.

Splash-plunk—splash-plunk—splash-plunk went Sandy's tail as he wagged it against the water.

– 10 –

Rosie and
the Dog Next Door

"Tell me again," said Franny. "Tell me again about Sandy and the wading pool and how some lady had him and Mimi found him and then you and Skinny-bones and George brought him home."

"I've told you about a million times already," said Rosie.

"Tell me *again*," said Franny, and the grownups all laughed, the way Rosie thought they *always* laughed when Franny said something that wasn't even funny. But tonight Rosie didn't care. Tonight was special. Tonight they were all in Dawn O'Day's yard for a welcome-home-Sandy party. They sat on the grass and on folding chairs, eating hamburgers and drinking lemonade. Aunt Kate brought balloons, and Miss Scott made a sheet cake with "Sandy" and "Mimi" across the top in squiggly pink letters.

"Maybe one more time wouldn't hurt," said Mr. Riggs.

"Yeah, one more time," said Franny.

"Well . . ." said Rosie, secretly glad to be telling the story again. "First we looked everywhere—Skinny-bones and I. And then we found George, and he told us about Sandy coming over the fence."

"And about the chocolate doughnut," said George.

"Yes," said Dawn O'Day, "and I've already called about getting a higher fence—and George has promised not to tempt Sandy with chocolate dough-nuts ever again. Right, George?"

"Right," said George, reaching for another piece of cake.

"Then we looked some more," said Rosie.

"And went down by the swimming pool," said Skinny-bones.

"And tried to think of where to look next."

"That's when I said we should look in *back* yards," said George.

"And we did," said Rosie, "and there still wasn't any Sandy, and we were just standing there, out on the sidewalk, and Mimi started pulling and barking the way she does, and we went around this house, and there he was. Ta-dum—in a wading pool."

"Tell about the lady who had him," said Franny.

"She didn't exactly *have* him," said Rosie. "He was just sort of *there*. And after we found him, this lady came out of her house and said how her children had been out in the yard and this dog— Sandy—wandered in and started playing with them for an excruciatingly long time. Then she and the children went inside to get shoes so they could go look for where Sandy lived, and that's when he climbed in the wading pool."

"And made his tail go 'splash-plunk,' " said Skinny-bones.

"And then we got there," said Rosie.

"And brought him home," said George.

"And now we're here," said Rosie, not wanting to let go of the tag end of the story, even though her father was raising his eyebrows as if to say "That's enough," and she could tell her mother and Aunt Kate wanted to clean up.

Later, after everything had been put away and Miss Scott, Aunt Kate, and Mr. and Mrs. Riggs had gone along home, Rosie, Skinny-bones, and Franny sat on the front porch with Sandy and Dawn O'Day. They listened to the sound of crickets and watched as George rode his bike, doing figure eights and bouncing over curbs, pulling up onto his back wheel as it screeched against the street. They saw the shadows on the grass and the trees across the street looming tall and dark.

"It's been a long day," said Miss O'Day. "For *us* and for Sandy."

"And Mimi, too," said Rosie, remembering how

Mimi had pulled at the leash and dragged them back to find Sandy.

"And Mimi, too," said Miss O'Day. She reached down and scratched Mimi behind the ears, then turned to pat the sleeping Sandy.

"Maybe he's dreaming about what he did all day," said Skinny-bones.

"Maybe," said Dawn O'Day. "Maybe so."

"Tell the Sandy story again," said Franny.

"I did," said Rosie. "About a billion times already."

"Come *on*," said Franny.

And Rosie started in again. She told about going up one block and down another; about talking to the mailman and the boy delivering meat for Meyer's Meat Market; about finding George. When she got to the part about Sandy in the wading pool, Franny yawned and rubbed her eyes. She went off the porch and onto the front yard, reaching for lightning bugs, catching them and letting them go.

Rosie watched her sister for a while, and then she went on. "You should've seen that wading pool," she said. "It was bigger than the one Sandy has here, wider, and not very deep. But it was green and sort of like the sea."

"Like a pirates' cove?" said Miss O'Day, leaning forward so that her rocking chair creaked against the floor.

"Yes," said Rosie. "That's it, a pirates' cove."

"With land curving all around?" said Miss O'Day. "And beaches. And farther back there were cliffs."

"And caves, too," said Rosie.

"For the pirates to hide in, and keep their treasure in," said Skinny-bones, wrapping her arms around her legs and pulling them close.

"There were toy boats," said Rosie.

"Sailing ships," said Dawn O'Day. "With masts tall as the sky and sails catching at the wind."

"And a plastic fish," said Rosie.

"It was a crocodile," said Skinny-bones. "With jaws that snapped."

"And it circled all around where the children were," said Rosie.

The streetlights went on up and down the street. George called, "Good night," and rode off around the corner. Franny did a handstand and then went along home. Crickets sang, and Sandy stirred and sat up, looking out toward the street.

"Because there *were* children, you know," Rosie went on. "Two girls and a boy. With a little black dog named Mimi. And they'd all been captured by pirates—"

"With wooden legs and patches on their eyes," added Skinny-bones.

"Who were nefarious *and* cantankerous," said Rosie.

"And then Sandy came," said Dawn O'Day. "And he found them, and dragged up pieces of wood,

and watched as they built a raft, and swam beside them all the way out to his ship, which was anchored at the mouth of the cove."

"They went up the rope ladder—even Sandy, even Mimi—and onto the ship." Rosie looked at the streetlamp and caught her breath. "And they sailed away by the light of the moon."

"All the way home," said Miss O'Day.

And on the porch, next to Rosie, Sandy the Super Dog growled softly and seemed to nod, his great head going up and down as if to say, "Yes—yes. I remember. Surely that's the way it was."